I0673346

Heaven's Window

Bill Selvitelle

Heaven's Window, published March, 2022

Editorial and proofreading services: Cath Lauria; Karen Grennan
Interior layout and cover design: Howard Johnson
Photo Credits: Front cover: "man, hugging, pet, sitting, street painting, Graffiti..." piqsels.com-id-fktew.jpg; "Bell Tower in the Evening light," ©Tess Turner, https://pixels.com/featured/bell-tower-in-the-evening-light-tess-turner.html

Author Photo: Owned by Bill Selvitelle

 **SDP Publishing**

Published by SDP Publishing, an imprint of SDP Publishing Solutions, LLC.

The characters, events, institutions, and organizations in this book are strictly fictional. Any apparent resemblance to any person, alive or dead, or to actual events is entirely coincidental.

All rights reserved. No part of the material protected by this copyright notice may be reproduced or utilized in any form or by any means, electronic or mechanical, including photocopying, recording, or by any information storage and retrieval system, without written permission from the copyright owner.

To obtain permission(s) to use material from this work, please submit a written request to:

SDP Publishing
Permissions Department
PO Box 26, East Bridgewater, MA 02333
or email your request to info@SDPPublishing.com.

ISBN-13 (print): 978-1-7378019-3-1
ISBN-13 (ebook): 978-1-7378019-4-8

Library of Congress Control Number: 2022900015

Copyright © 2022, Bill Selvitelle

Printed in the United States of America

First Printing

I want to acknowledge all the homeless souls that struggle each day. You are not alone, you are not forgotten, you are loved.

I want to thank my wife, Susan, and our son, Michael, for supporting me on this journey. Your support and love are amazing. I could not have done this without all your love.

Word from the Author

I worked for the local utility company for nearly forty years. In that time, I saw homeless people all around. When I could, I helped them out with money, food, and clothing. After I retired, I became a Yoga instructor. Not what I'd envisioned for the next chapter of my life, but life has a way of changing you.

One day, on a whim, I asked folks at the yoga studio to make up some kindness bundles—these are one-gallon zip-lock bags filled with snacks, socks, water, personal care items, and most important: a prayer, a note of encouragement, something to make that person feel a little better.

I received over a hundred kindness bundles and took them to Methadone Mile in Boston. My aim that day was to drop these off and be done with this adventure. Little did I know how I would be changed by this one interaction.

The first person I saw was a young man with his son walking down Topeka Street. It was a bitter cold morning, the temp not more than ten degrees when I pulled my car over, opened my trunk that was full of bundles, and handed him one. He was at first taken aback with the gift. His son, now on his shoulders, looked at the gifts inside. It was obvious to me that this man of no more than thirty and his son of around three were in need.

Tears filled the man's eyes as I handed him another bundle for his son. Trying to compose himself, he asked his son, "What do you say to the man?"

In a soft voice the child said, "Thank you, sir."

I would like to say that the cold air made my eyes well up but that would be a lie.

My mission grew to giving out every type of clothing you could think of, depending on the season. I would make four to five trips in a week to see my friends. Their need was great, and if I did not have a constant stream of kind and giving individuals my mission wouldn't have continued. I got help from hundreds of extremely generous people around the South Shore of Boston, along with friends and family all around the country.

I wanted, or better said, needed, to share my experiences with those that gave so much to help our brothers and sisters. The best way to explain the struggles and victories was through Facebook and Instagram. Every time I went into Boston and the surrounding towns, I tried to give a voice, a name, to so many people that have been left behind. My readers on social media have gotten to know our friend Michael at State and Congress, Melody and Leroy, and so many other men and women that live on the streets. This in turn made me want to write a story of one man's struggle with life.

Chapter 1

ON THE STREETS

Walking past the storefronts on this cold January morning, I can smell breakfast up ahead. I pause to listen to the church bells as they chime six, then stop for a moment longer to look at my reflection in the storefront window. My hair is greyer than I remembered, longer as well. Probably the longest it has ever been. I take off my warm wool hat and try to comb my hair with my fingers. I need a shave, and my grey beard needs adjustment. A short warm jacket covers my longer full-length brown coat. I laugh at how ridiculous I look. Nevertheless, dressing in layers is a must during the New England winters.

Many bums like me walk by, give a wave, or sometimes sit down and talk about their lives even when you wish they wouldn't. The conversation is almost always the same. How the government, life, friends have all let them down. They consider and validate each day that all the pain and suffering in their lives are somehow others' faults. We are just victims, unable to move on, even a little bit.

I think to myself as I listen to their drama, am I as bad as this? Am I like them? Have I become stuck in the world of handouts, has-beens, and the forgotten? I fool myself to believe this is only temporary.

Chapter 2

SUNSHINE

Sunshine and I have not eaten a square meal in a few days. There are times, days, when eating food and having enough clean water does not happen. Eating less and not feeling the pains of hunger is a lesson I learned in the war. I always try to make sure Sunshine eats well and has enough water to drink, though.

I keep her on a short leash when we walk on the sidewalks. There are too many people around; at times, she wants to jump and play with everyone. Like all dogs, she has the innate ability to love unconditionally.

We stop just before the cafeteria on Tremont Street, across from the Common. I search through my coat and pants pockets to see how much money I have. Eighteen cents; I laugh at myself as a few pennies slip from my cold hands onto the ground. I plop down next to Sunshine onto the freezing cold sidewalk, reach over for the pennies, take off my worn-out hat, and put them and the rest of my fortune inside. I pat her for a moment, close my eyes, and remember.

I first met my four-legged friend about two years ago in the Boston Common. My day's work was done, and to cap off the evening, a pleasant stroll was just what I needed. I'd watched as this beautiful mutt walked around by herself. As I paused to sit on a bench, I noticed how she would crouch down, real low to the ground, wagging her tail, and dash to get the squirrels. Fortunately for those furry rodents, they got away up the trees.

I smiled as I watched her a bit longer. She would be silly at times and have the most fun by chasing her own tail, but once caught, she would let it go. After a while, when she was tuckered out, she sat, licked her lips, and looked over at me. Her head tilted side to side as if she were asking me questions. Finally, I got up the nerve to call her over; she darted toward me in a flash.

She was lovely, medium build with a dark brown coat and a few white patches dotted all around. She had a wet, shiny brown nose, floppy ears, a short tail, and the kindest eyes you would ever see. She was wagging, dancing. It was as if she had found her best friend. Checking to see if she had a collar on, I was surprised that there was none.

I bent over to greet her, and as I did, she licked me all over my face. I smiled and laughed as I gave her a few kisses and patted her back. She plopped down next to my feet and leaned her body weight onto my legs. A few minutes passed before I decided that it was time to go home. Nudging my feet gently under her body, she sprang up, licked her lips, and smiled at me. It was time for dinner; the night was on its way. I had only a few blocks to go to get to my apartment in the West End.

Wishing my new friend a good night, I patted her head and told her, "Head home, find your family." I was not more than twenty-five feet away when I felt a nudge at my right leg. It was the dog. Leaning down, I looked into her eyes and spoke again.

"Girl, you need to go home. I can't have pets at my place."

She looked unimpressed at my answer. A few whimpers and a lick of her lips told me that my friend was hungry. I looked around the Common; most people who had been seated on the benches were gone, and only a few travelers came and went out of the park. No one seemed to be looking for their dog. I waited for a few minutes and then said, "Okay, pretty girl, let's get you some food."

We walked slowly together. I had no way of holding onto the dog. I was a bit anxious that she would run out into the street. "Okay, girl, sit here," I said in a loud, somewhat commanding voice. "Let's wait for the traffic to pass." She sat properly and was relaxed. It was as if she knew about traffic and commands. But before we crossed, a quick glance back to the Common had no one coming to or calling her.

We crossed the road to the nearest food store. I asked her to "sit here and be good, I will be right out." She smiled at me as if she understood.

Most of the local food stores around Boston are run by Irish and Italian families. In this location, on Tremont Street, it was an Italian family that ran the food store.

I needed to make this quick so I could get back to the dog. An older and quite round Italian woman dressed all in black stood behind the register.

"Excuse me, sorry, where is the dog food?" I asked in a hurried tone. The lady looked puzzled. It was now time for charades. I pointed to my legs, two, and then made my hand for four, then pointed to my backside wagging my imaginary tail. "Dog food."

In her broken English, she said, "You mean Alpo, Alpoa?"

I smiled, trying not to laugh. "alpha," I said. "Where is that, on what aisle?" She pointed to aisle three. I grabbed a few cans and hurried to the counter.

"You geta new cane?" the lady from behind the counter asked.

A cane, no ... what does she mean by a cane? A walking cane?

The lady's arms and hands started to move about quickly. "A new cane, woof, woof. Ah, how you say, a new dog?"

I smiled at her as I said, "Well, yes, sort of. I'm not sure." I was getting impatient with this event.

The lady spoke Italian under her breath as she rang up my fare and placed the cans in a brown paper bag. "Thank you," I said and quickly went outside. My new friend was waiting, smiling; she knew I had dinner for her. Taking one can out of the paper bag, I realized I needed a can opener.

"Okay, girl, let's be off," I said to her as I scanned the Common and streets for her owner. I thought it a bit odd that no one was looking for this beautiful mutt. As I patted her head she sprang up from her seated position, wagged her tail in a frenzied manner, and smiled at me. She stayed close by my side as we began our walk.

My thoughts went to how could I get her back to Howard Street into my studio apartment without being noticed. *What the heck. Let us give it a try;* maybe no one will be around to turn me in.

Walking up Tremont Street, we paused for a quick look into the trash cans that sat at the curb. I needed to find a rope to use as a makeshift collar and leash. Looking around on the sidewalk and street for something to keep my new friend safe, I spied a long piece of packing rope on the sidewalk up ahead. Making a collar of sorts with one part of the rope, I placed it gently over her head. She wasn't resistant to having one on. Fortunately, there was enough left over for a short leash.

We quietly made our way to the third floor of the five-story walk-up without anyone seeing us. My key rattled into the lock as the dog danced next to me. She was excited!

She darted to the living room and sat up tall and proud as I went to the cupboard and found one of the two bowls that I had. Placing the dog food and bowl on the counter, I searched my messy junk draw for the can opener. "Yup, I've got to clean that drawer out someday," I said to myself.

Slowly opening the can, the smell of dog food encompassed the whole kitchen; it was disgusting. Filling the bowl halfway with the smelly food, I put it down on the floor. My friend wasted no time devouring all that was there. I took the other bowl and filled it with water from the kitchen tap. "Girl, you can have the rest later. I don't want you getting sick."

She moved her head side to side and licked her lips, then slowly went over to the bowl of water. Unfortunately, in her haste to drink, most of the water splashed onto the floor. I smiled at her as I heard the church bells chime seven.

I had my dinner and sat quietly reading the newspaper until it was nearly time for bed. Rain had begun to fall, but I needed, or better said, she needed to get out to do her business. Putting on her leash, I grabbed my coat and headed quietly down the back stairs and out the back door into the small courtyard. This was a fenced-in area, where she couldn't run away. I stood in the doorway as she sniffed the air, then made a dash behind a tree. She returned, wagging her tail and soaking wet.

I whispered, "Come on, girl, let's get upstairs, dry you off, and get some shut-eye."

Dashing up the flights of stairs, she ran straight into my apartment; it was as if she had lived here before. She danced and pranced on the wooden floors in the happiest of ways. "Okay girl, relax, you can't be making all that noise. The neighbors downstairs will surely hear your nails on the floor."

Calming her down, I grabbed a big towel from the closet and dried her off as well as possible. She grinned and wagged, clearly feeling, maybe for the first time in a long time, safe and warm. Rummaging around in the bottom of the bedroom closet, I found a couch blanket. It smelled of old mothballs, and to be sure, I had never cleaned this article before. Thinking for a moment, I was not quite sure this was even mine. Most likely it had been left by the previous tenant.

As I folded it into a makeshift bed, it wasn't hard to tell that it had seen better days, but this would do for my house guest. She curled up onto the blanket after I finished up drying her off. I had a feeling of joy in having a guest in my humble home. I sat comfortably in my parlor chair with my coffee and began to read the Record American newspaper. I hadn't read much more than the headline on the front page when I fell fast asleep.

Early the next morning, bright rays burst through the windows, so bright that at first it was hard to see. I squinted and looked around to find my friend was next to me on the floor, sleeping. For a second I thought it was a dream, that last night hadn't happened; there was no way I had a dog in my life. Then I heard her yawn and saw her lick her lips.

"Yup," I said under my breath, "I have a dog." I laughed and smiled.

I looked at her for a few minutes and pondered what I should do. It was then that I realized that the morning sunshine had shifted just enough to cover my new friend in light. Closing my eyes for a moment, I rested my head back against the seat and thought, *Sunshine, that is what I will call her.*

I surveyed my apartment. The fresh sunlight opened my eyes to the dull, drab walls, and worn-out, water-stained hardwood floors. I kept my home clean, but you would never really know to look at how shabby the place was. Most men my age had families, homes in the suburbs, good-paying jobs with prospects for more. I had a few pictures of my family on the wall, and one from my outfit in the Marines. Other than those the walls were empty— well, sort of. The outlines of previous tenants' frames on the walls highlighted the faded wallpaper around them where priceless works of art may have hung.

I struggled each week to survive. Work was work, boring but it paid the bills. It was a living wage, sort of. Sometimes I tried to save for a rainy day, but they never stayed saved for long.

I never asked for assistance from anyone though, especially the state. I'd learned that lesson from my mom and dad, to not be on the dole.

So many thoughts were swimming in my head. I had no real girlfriends to speak of. A date and dance at the Peabody club here and there, but not much more. It was hard to court a girl when your funds were always low.

Somehow, I knew deep inside that if I'd had a chance with Cathy, I would have pushed myself to be something more.

I was behind on the rent—three weeks late, to be precise. It looked like I would be evicted any day. I had seen the notice to "quit the premises" on the doors of other tenants through the years. The scuttlebutt was that this person or that family had skipped out in the dark of night, still owing back rent. I hated the idea of doing such a thing. It was not who I was, nor was it the way I had been raised.

With few options left though, I had little choice; it was about survival. The little I had saved would now carry me to a lesser home. Not as safe, not as clean, but I'd still have a roof over my head, or so I thought.

So many times I had looked at the bums on the street and wondered what happened to them to make them become beggars. I was afraid that I might be like them, the bums who live on the streets one day.

I convinced myself that it would never happen to me. *This will be a transition to a new start. I have a new friend—someone to talk to, who doesn't ask anything but a pat on the head and a can of food.*

It was time for work. I snuck Sunshine once again down the back stairs to the courtyard for her morning business. Then, in a flash, we were back upstairs. I could hear people beginning their day, and I had to be on my way as well.

"Okay, girl, you be good and please don't bark, or we will surely be in trouble." Sunshine nodded as if she understood; she curled up on her blanket in the middle of the floor in a warm patch of sun.

Chapter 3

MOVING

I grew up in Boston—well, all around Boston. My family moved from East Boston to South Boston, then to Dorchester and Roxbury. The family was made up of just the three of us—my parents and me—which made it easy to move when we had to. We were not poor, but we weren't even close to middle class either. Mom would always mend my jeans and shirts when they got ripped. Outgrowing things was the only time that I got new clothing. We never went hungry, though. There was food enough for everyone, a roof over our head, and church on Sunday. We lived a simple, happy life.

Friends and schoolmates came and went. With all the moving I found it difficult to fit in, especially after my father passed away suddenly. I was only twelve when he died from a heart attack. For a time, friends and neighbors came around to give support, a meal, a phone call. Then, as quick as they all came, it seemed they all disappeared just as fast.

"That's life," my mom would say, "we have to move on and start anew each morning." Mom was never the same after dad passed. Her smile, her true smile, left her. She would put on a brave face for me and those she met on the street, but I could see her pain. She tried, but she could not hide it from me. After dinner, she often just sat and looked out the parlor and kitchen windows for hours. It seemed to me as if she was waiting and looking for Dad to be walking down the street, coming home. Most of the time she sat silently, but once in a while she would whisper a song and softly cry.

It was now just Mom and me. I had to be in charge, help more around the house, get any odd job I could to make a few dollars. We moved one more time, finally settling in a two-bedroom apartment in the Hyde Park section of Boston at the end of a dead-end street that abutted the train tracks. Not the best of locations, but the rent was cheap.

It took about six months for Mom to get out of the doldrums. She found a job as a seamstress at a local factory three blocks away. I was happy for her. The job gave her purpose and the much-needed money for us to survive. Mom kept us off government assistance. We made a simple life even simpler for ourselves, until the Nazis invaded Poland.

I was seventeen when war broke out in the world. I wanted to join up and fight then, even though America was not at war yet. Everyone knew it was only a matter of time before we would be fighting the Nazis or Mussolini in Europe, though.

Mom would not let me sign up for the service until I was eighteen. The day after my birthday, I signed up with the Marines. I could not wait to serve my country. I convinced Mom that we would most likely not even get into the war, but that was a white lie. I wanted to be ready to serve, and that way I could also send her money to help out around the house. None of this mattered to her. She was upset, thinking I would get hurt, or worse, killed.

Heading off on the train from South Station to Paris Island, South Carolina, for training, we said our good-byes. The next day the Japs hit Pearl Harbor, and we were *all* in the war.

THE WEST END

I never lived in the West End as a child, only on my own as an adult. The area was a mixture of all races and creeds. Not like the North End and East Boston, which was all Italian. South Boston was all Irish. Roxbury was black and Hispanic. Dorchester was a mix of Irish and Italian. In the West End white, black, Jews, Catholics, Italians, and Irish seemed to get along and live peaceful lives.

The world had changed faster than ever. When I found the last of my three apartments in nineteen fifty-seven, the West End was on its last legs. Boston was moving to new beginnings. The newspapers herald stories of what the West End of Boston would become. It was time for a change in the city. "*A bright new future awaits.*" Billboard signs promised a new beginning for the residents after this area was razed.

A few opposition groups had sprung up to stop the development. No one was fooling themselves though; the winds of change had come. Soon a new city hall, modern office buildings, high rise apartments, open spaces and parks would be here. Such an ambitious plan had never been offered before in this city.

I thought to myself *I bet dollars to donuts this new plan does not include any part of Beacon Hill.* All the so-called Blue Bloods or the Brahmins called that part of the city home.

There is a saying in Boston:

> *And this is good old Boston,*
> *The home of the bean and the cod,*
> *Where the Lowells talk only to Cabots,*
> *And the Cabots talk only to God.*

The upper class, I am sure, spent many nights watching the West End shows. The West End was the place to see any hit show when it came to Boston. There was a time when it was fashionable for people around Boston to go to the "Old Howard" or the Olympian. You could once have seen a Shakespeare play performed by the "Booth Brothers." Yes, the infamous John Wilkes Booth. As time passed into the twentieth century, many Hollywood stars played the West End.

The West End began to fall on hard times after the Second World War. It became more of a transient part of the town. Families left for safer areas for their kids to grow up in. As the years rolled on, the West End went downhill. Strip joints, gin mills, prostitution, and crime became more and more a fact of everyday life. Once Vaudeville had had its place, then the movies were the draw, and finally, striptease shows became their demise.

The wrecking ball was here, and it was going to take me down with it.

Chapter

WORK

I was late for work again. As always seemed to be the way when you are late for anything, everything else was late as well. This morning the bus and trains had been running behind schedule.

As I rushed into the factory, the workday had already begun. The shop was in full swing, and the noise of metal being bent, cut, crunched, and pounded filled the air. Trying to quietly punch my timecard outside the office, the thud of my time clock summoned the boss's secretary, Nancy. She opened her door and calmly said, "Mr. Buford would like to see you in his office right now." I could tell by Nancy's voice that I was in trouble.

I knocked gently on Mr. Buford's door.

"Come in," his cold voice shouted.

There are lots of times in life when you know what is coming. It is a look, a feel at that moment. They are never generally good outcomes. I had a bad feeling that such would be the case today. It is certainly not the feeling of having a winner at the track. You know, when the horses are in the gate, the flag goes up, bells ring, and they are

24

off. You hear the sounds of thundering hoof beats coming down the stretch and just know that your horse will win.

This was not that feeling. My horse had come up lame.

I stood in front of Mr. Buford's oversized, ornately carved desk and stared blankly as he read my file out loud to me. I already knew the outcome. *Let us get on with this*, I thought to myself. Yes, Mr. Buford was correct that my work had been less than good.

"Mistakes, so many careless mistakes." He went on to read all my shortcomings and the cost of each one.

"What happened to you?" Mr. Burford asked in a concerned voice, not really caring for an answer. I let him continue. I thought the same, after all: what has happened to me?

Mr. Burford brought the hammer down next.

"I'm sorry, but we just can't employ you here at our plant anymore. The risks for you and the company are too high. I've seen this many times before. Men get bored or find out that this job is no longer for them."

Looking right at him, I smiled. He was correct that my passion for this line of work was now gone. It was time to move on, in so many ways.

"I am giving you two weeks' pay, plus what you have coming for vacation money." Mr. Buford looked down at his ledger. As his phone began to ring, he let it go until his secretary in the outer room answered for him. "I am sure you will find another line of work, or maybe you can go back to school?"

I nodded slightly as Mr. Buford went from chastising me to giving me friendly advice.

I did thank him for the years of employment, knowing all too well that pleading for another chance would be futile. The truth be told, I was happy, or better put, my feeling was relief to be free from a job that no longer worked for me. I was still relativity young. I could find a better job with more money. Who knew, maybe even enough to go on a proper date. Besides that, I had Sunshine—a new beginning with a new friend.

Wishing Mr. Buford well, I took the brown pay packet with my cash, shook his hand, and walked out of his office.

Nancy already knew my fate. Her desk was placed in the outer office so that she could hear every conversation above a whisper.

I smiled confidently at her; she seemed a bit taken aback by me not looking upset.

"I won't be but a minute. I want to get my belongings out of my locker and then I will drop you back the key."

Nancy smiled, looked down at her typewriter, and went back to work without saying a word.

The plant was running along, machines still crunching metal and the whirring noises of other devices filled the air. Men were at their trade, their stations. No one saw what had happened to me. Little did I know that this would be my first step to becoming invisible, a feeling that would soon be part of my life.

I grabbed the few clothing articles I had from my locker, dropped back the key to Nancy, smiled at her again, and walked out the door.

There were no trains or busses to catch; no need to rush. Walking back home that morning in a daze, I wondered what I might do next. About halfway home, I suddenly remembered that I had a new friend waiting for me.

The unemployment office could wait to see me another day. I had a spring in my step again. I hadn't noticed before now that it had disappeared. I had someone in my life to begin anew, even if she had four legs and a tail. Sunshine would be happy to see me.

It also hit me that I was being responsible for another being. The feeling of having a dog in my life filled my soul with joy.

By the time I reached my building, the morning was nearly done. The street was quiet, everyone at work or having lunch. Only one car was on Howard Street, about one hundred yards away. It did not appear to be the landlord's vehicle. The only activity was the ice man's truck in front of our building.

Our local ice guy came around the West End three times a week, mostly at midday when the housewives were home. Some tenants had refrigerators, but most had the ice man make deliveries. My ice came on Saturday. I tried to make it last the week, but it usually didn't. Looking up on the windows that faced Howard Street, I could see the ice placards in the window telling the man how many people needed blocks.

One of the two ice delivery guys shouted to me, "Do you need any ice today?"

Smiling back, I replied, "Nope, I'm good."

Going into my pocket, I found my house keys and crept upstairs. *The landlord may be around later today looking to catch me and other tenants at home and press us for our back rent.* Sometimes the landlord would go into the apartments to see if you were packing up to leave. He usually did that under the guise of checking for a leaking pipe or a smell of gas. *I wondered if he parked his car on the back streets so he would not be noticed.*

I approached my front door very quietly. The outside wooden floorboards creaked as I placed one foot in front of the other. Funny, I never remember hearing them creak before. Placing my right ear to the wooden door, I listened for any noise. *Was Sunshine sleeping? Had she ripped my stuff apart? What type of mess was awaiting me? Was the landlord inside?* So many thoughts swirled in my head.

Quietly, I put the key into the lock. As I turned the knob, the door hinges let me know that oil was needed. I slowly pushed the door open, not knowing what was waiting for me.

To my delight, about three feet from the door was Sunshine. She sat up tall, tilting her head to one side as if she were asking, "Where have you been?"

Feeling my face smile larger than it had in an exceptionally long time, I fell to the floor and gave her a big hug. Sunshine danced, twirled in the happiest of ways. *What a crazy day.* I'd lost my job and now I was rolling around on the floor with a dog that I hardly knew.

After a few minutes of fun, reality and anxiety crept in. We both stopped playing around. I sat up on the floor as Sunshine came next to me, plopping her head on my right leg, her brown eyes looking up at me. Just then everything that had happened today truly hit me. I whispered to Sunshine, "What are we going to do, girl?" The bells at the church rang at noon.

Sunshine and I had the most wonderful of afternoons that day; we ate all the food we could. Then I put on the radio so we could listen to some music as I settled into the parlor chair. I knew this was the end of era for me.

My mind was spinning; my belly felt uneasy. I was exhausted, the emotions of sadness replaced with joy to be met again by fear. Then, in only a minute, I was asleep, and my dreams took me back to the Pacific.

Chapter

WAR

I realized early on that when you were in battle, you never really knew where you were, not that it mattered much. So long as you weren't on the other side of the line, at least. One foxhole looked like another; every trench, gully, or tree was the same. The only difference was how much blood had been left behind. It could have been ours, or theirs. Each day we advanced a mile or more, to hold, retreat, hold, then move. We scattered left, then right a hundred yards, crawling on our bellies or hunched over. Slipping in and out trying to outfox the enemy was a daunting challenge.

All we wanted to do was win the war and go home without any damage to our bodies or mind. That was sadly not the case for many of us. If you made it home, you brought back baggage that you'd never expected to have. I tried not to complain; after all, we were the lucky ones that made it back.

I came to the sad realization early on in the war that my hearing was going. The deafening sounds of all types of weapons ruined your ears. It seemed like we heard them constantly. The long-range guns from the ships would startle you during the first volley. Then came the loud "boom" from far away and the whistle of the projectile racing overhead a second or two later, then a seismic shake of the earth as it landed. It always made my stomach drop. The screams of men not yet dead would fill the air, and then silence would take hold.

In the beginning, when shells from the ships' guns or artery fire would land close to us, my backside would pucker up and my stomach would drop. In short order though, we all got used to that feeling and noise.

The close-contact small arms, rifle, and machine gun noise got so bad all of us took the filters off our cigarette rations and stuck them in our ears. A low hum became my constant companion.

It rained wherever I was. It was never a hard, driving rain, but the kind of rain that came down straight and poured on you each afternoon and for most of the nights. As hard as you tried to stay dry, you eventually gave up the ghost and became one with always being wet.

As wet as I was, I never felt clean. All of us constantly sweated, even when we were sitting doing nothing. Sweat would roll down our backs, faces, and everywhere else. Mosquitoes, gnats, and other types of flying and crawling bugs bit constantly. The sound of men slapping skin was always around. Even when you tried to make it a quiet slap, it never worked.

When it came time for our unit to come off the line for a day, one of the first things we did after getting good chow was jump in the ocean to bathe.

Being still and silent was a must when you were on the point. Each movement of a branch, a crack of a twig made in front of you put you on edge. My eyes were always ready to tell my brain to let my finger know it was okay to pull the trigger on my M1 Carbine. Most of the time the noise was an animal, bird, or insect. You found out real fast if it was the enemy. We all saw firsthand the hard reality that it could be one of our men, someone lost, or maybe finding a place to go to the bathroom.

We were on the Peleliu Island for about a month when one of the worst days of the war happened. Our unit was assigned to accompany another section of Marines. This gave us about fifty bodies for special operation. Our job was to find out where a reported Jap radio transmitter might be. We were to kill or capture the enemy and find the radio equipment before it could be destroyed. If we were successful, we might get off the island a lot quicker.

A zig-zag line formed as we went out into the thick jungle. You wanted to be able to see the Marine over to your left and right if you were in the center. The guys on the zig and zag made sure to keep a watch for their counterparts too. We tried to keep about ten yards in front of each other. It was not always an easy task, as the thick undergrowth made the journey difficult. There were times when you lost sight of the Marine you were following.

We were about an hour or so into the mission when a single shot rang out. Everyone ducked for cover and waited for the return fire. Was it a sniper? Laying in the prone position gun at the ready, we all looked to see if any advance by the enemy was heading our way. Time slowly ticked, and it felt like an hour before we rose up. Slowly, with a heightened sense of life and death, we walked in the direction of where the sound came from.

It was an awful sight to see. A Marine from the other squad had shot one of our guys. We were not sure how

John had gotten so far away from the line. I stared for a moment at John's lifeless body. He was shot through the forehead, a clean shot. The small bullet wound did not look much in the front, but the back of his head was missing.

The Marine who had shot John was inconsolable. He was crying, screaming. A few of the other Marines took him out of the line and brought him back to camp. The guys in our unit were very upset. Our CO took control after a minute, barking out orders to bring John back and for others to get on the point. I gathered John's weapon and slung in onto my back. Our mission was not over.

I made some good friends in the war. You needed them, and they needed you. A trust, a bond, was formed between you. John's demise brought us all closer.

I met men from all around the country. When we had some down time, we sat around and told tales of where we were from. Most all of them talked differently than I did. They all thought my accent was odd. I'd never thought I had one until someone pointed out my "car parked in Harvard Yard." That always got a laugh.

Everyone talked of home, families, their girl or wife, and kids. I did the same. The two years plus I was in were hell. All I wanted was to be home with my mom and start a family with Cathy. That, as it turned out, would not be.

I awoke with a start, my heart racing. I knew that I had been having nightmares of the war. Jumping up from my chair, I startled Sunshine a bit, and she jumped up as well. I looked all around the apartment. How sad this was living in a place I didn't care for, with none of my old friends around anymore. The sunlight, my Sunshine, had shone a new light on my life. It was time to leave— to make a fresh start with my new friend. I patted my thighs. "Come on, girl."

Reaching under the bed, I pulled out my suitcase. I plopped it onto the bed, flung it open, and filled it with all that I would need—one suit, socks, underwear, shaving kit, blanket, and my pillow. I tossed in a few other items as I cleaned out the place. The rest of what I had would be left for the next soul to take over. Maybe he would have better luck.

Snapping the two latches on my case, I gathered up the leash.

"Come on, Sunshine. We have a world to explore." She leaped up, kissing me as if she knew we were off on an adventure.

Chapter 7

TRANSITION

I had no real plan on what I would do for a job, and pounding the pavement every day got to be very discouraging. Months and months of getting "no's" or "try here or there" for a job led me to feel depressed. It got to be that within just a few minutes, I could look at the person doing the interview and know that no position was available for me. My eyes glazed over as the same speech came my way again and again.

Lots of jobs, factory work, was already in Japan. More and more labor was being sent overseas. Cheap labor was becoming a way of life in the world. The few jobs that were around were in high demand.

"Unfortunately, we don't have anything for you right now." Each company had a different way of telling you that you were not wanted.

My savings would not last much longer. Sunshine and I had managed to stay at low-rent flophouses around the city so far. These places gave you a roof over your head, and somewhat of a clean room. Each room had a sink in the parlor, a hot plate if you were lucky, and the bathroom was always down the hall. The little money that I had left would soon be gobbled up by finding places to live.

I had considered going back to school on the G.I. bill, but how would I support myself if I were in college? What if I failed at going back to school? I convinced myself that later down the road school would be an option, just not now.

Each time Sunshine and I moved to lesser abodes, the sadder I got. Every day my goal was simply for both of us to have one good meal, and to find a job. Oh, how I longed to be someone else. I would love to reinvent myself, just as I had when I went into the service. Would welfare be my last safety net?

A black suit, white shirt, and black shoes were my uniform each day. Having a warm overcoat filled out my ensemble. Two clean outfits were a must; in fact, they were the same black suit. I bought them in Filene's Basement, where everything was always on sale. When one suit needed to be cleaned, my spare would keep me in the game. I left Sunshine safe in the apartment while I went around looking for work.

Eventually though, trying less or giving up altogether became more the norm than looking for work. I would wander the West End and all around the Boston streets during the day. Walking in good or bad weather gave me a chance to clear my mind and investigate the storefront windows for anyone hiring. Most nights I ended up at one of the local bars for a beer with some kind of dinner.

As I walked the streets, day after day, I found myself getting more and more discouraged. In time I found the local watering holes that opened at eight in the morning. These establishments tended to the working men who had overnight shift work. They were in fact, a haven for all like me who had no place to be.

Finding friends at bars was easy when you had money for drinks. So many men, war vets like me, found a place—a second home, if you will—at the bar. We showed up when it opened and some of us stayed till it closed at night. There are so many reasons why bars become a way of life. The loss of a job, family, divorce, jail, fighting— pretty much anything and everything meant finding a way to the pub. It became effortless to fall into this displaced world—too easy, in fact.

Some of the finer establishments put out a lunch spread—rolls you could fill with ham, cheese, bologna. Once in a while, even roast beef would be there. Such a treat. Of course, this was to get you to buy more beer and whiskey to wash the food down. I would partake in the feast of eating and drinking with ease. Before the lunch spread was taken away, I would gather up an extra sandwich for my girl.

Days went into weeks that turned into months. When I began my trek, it was February; now, it was April. The few friends and couple of cousins I kept in contact with were moving on in their lives, while I was stuck in the past. I stopped calling after my mother passed; it had been almost two years since the cancer took her.

It was easy, as sad as that sounds, not to talk to those you were once close with. They all had jobs, families. I was tired of hearing about all the good in their lives. When anyone asked about me, my white lies were always in play.

When Mom was alive and not too sick with cancer, we would try to make it over to a family party, birthday, anniversary, or a cookout. I had no car, so begging a ride was always an issue. The commuter rail worked to a point, although I had to make sure we left early enough to catch the last train out. Sometimes getting to the celebration was too much work, and we would make excuses as to why we could not come—more white lies, if you will.

Mom and I would make a point to be at Christmas Eve with whomever of the family members had enough space to host a dinner, though. It truly was a great time to see family, to give and receive presents and connect with people, most of whom you had not seen or heard from since the last holiday. Mom and I never held any such gatherings.

Thinking back, other than my mom coming over to my place a few times, I'd never had family over to my apartment. I felt it suitable for a long time to hear good stories about the ones in my life. Now I was beyond that. The trips to Warren Bank would not be needed for coins to make phone calls any longer.

Chapter 8

GIVING UP

My last attempt at finding work was perhaps a blessing in disguise. I was at the bar when it opened at eight in the morning. A cold draft beer and pickled eggs were my breakfast as I scanned the Boston Globe and Herald Traveler help wanted ads. This was now my routine: get up, take care of Sunshine, put on my suit, head to the bar. Sometimes I would bring Sunshine and read the newspaper employment section—no need to walk the city in search of work. This day, thankfully, I'd kept her home.

I whispered softly to myself as I read, "Looking for a motivated salesman to sell the new product line. No experience necessary; will train. Apply at 900 Washington Street, Boston, from 12-5 today. See Mr. Johnson, second floor.

"Yes, yes," I spoke confidently to myself. "This is the one." I downed my beer. "Jim." I pointed to the bartender to come over. "One shot of Jameson, please. Look at this." I gestured to the paper for Jim to see. "Here's the thing, Jim. I have a chance at a job."

Jim took the white rag off his shoulder and began

to wipe the bar where I was. "You have a job interview today?" he said it a disbelieving voice.

"Yes. If I hurry, I can be one of the first in line. Who knows, this might be my ticket back." I was so excited. It felt like when I had a winner at the racetrack. A sure thing, could not lose.

Looking back on Jim's face, I should have seen this coming.

"Thanks so much for listening," I said. Looking into the mirror behind the bar, I stood up straight, dusted off my suit, and headed off. I thought I looked good; better yet, I felt alive.

Chapter *9*

BEGGING

Sunshine sits next to me, her face smiling, tongue out. I smile as she begins to lick my running nose—a few people who pass by look down and make their crude remarks at what has just happened. Then, finally, I put my hand out and ask, "Can you spare a dime?"

The first time I said those words, I remembered an old Bugs Bunny cartoon. I do not know much about that storyline—I was, after all, just a kid—but I could see it so clearly. During the cartoon, a disheveled Humphry Bogart walked up to Bugs and asked, "Hey buddy, can you stake a fellow American who's down on his luck?" Bugsy reached into his pocket, found a coin, tossed it, and then told him to scram. I felt it was harsh even then for Bugs to act that way.

My hand and hat are out again as a few more people walk by. I look up, and as I do, I see a couple of ladies coming toward me. Once they see me, they clutch their pocketbooks closer to their bodies. In a flash, they swing them to the other side away from me. I smile and ask, "Can you spare—"

Before I can finish, they are away. Then, thinking

out loud, I whisper to Sunshine, "What did they think, I was going to jump up and rob them?" Sunshine is not impressed with my speech. She curls up and lays down next to me, knowing all too well we may be here for a while. The delicious smell of eggs, bacon, and fresh coffee swirl all around the street, making both our stomachs ache for food.

My right hand stays at the ready, palm up, glad for my left to meet it when anyone comes by. The morning passes slow. The frozen ground is making my bottom ache. I take off my small jacket and place it under my backside. I often just sit and watch the world go by—the cars and busses all with a destination in mind. I do not constantly beg; I find it to be exhausting. Park Street Church bells chime eight, and their sounds wake me out of my haze.

"Can you help me, anything?"

My left arm is outstretched now, giving my right arm a break. So often, people will drop cigarettes on me as if they do not see me sitting here. I can tell they do it on purpose. The worst thing is when people spit at you. It happens more often than you would think. The long inhale through the nose, catching all the phlegm they have, and then *splat* somewhere near me. Not too many other things you can sit next to that will turn your stomach like that.

Every now and then, a cup of warm coffee and a donut will find me via a kind person on his or her way to or from work. Even when I make a good haul of cash, begging takes part of my soul.

When the crowds of people thin out, I close my eyes and think about forming a plan to get off the street, with the hope of finding a job and a place to again call my own. I get mad at myself for not doing more. Why am I stuck here at the bottom rung of society? I could, I thought, move back into the world of the living. I felt so ashamed of myself for not doing it. As hard as it is to be a bum, a beggar, it's so much more difficult to get off the street The invisible pull of staying homeless keeps me chained down.

I can feel at times that my mind slips away when the deep sadness is overwhelming. If it were not for Sunshine I would have given up. She is the bright light, my joy, my sunshine. She keeps madness away.

Chapter *10*

FREEDOM

Our first day on the streets felt no different than any other day, except for the fact that I now had a companion. Someone I was responsible for. It felt wonderful to have a friend.

My cash and my bank book were safely tucked into my shirt pocket. Before we left our last flat, I checked to see my balance: $137.42. My cash money was $38.75. It was sad to see that this was my entire life's monetary worth. Yet, all-in-all, I felt like a million dollars; I was free from the shackles of the apartment. Free from looking for work, for a while at least. I could breathe again.

Seeing homeless men around all these years, I knew that they slept in doorways, on park benches, and in the subway. They somehow survived. But were they truly free? My concern for now was the inclement weather, rain, and cold. I would not think about the winter. That was two seasons away, so who knows what and where Sunshine and I would be? After all, we would have a home by then.

One night turned into the next. We woke up early, usually when the dawn broke. Another alarm that woke us up was the sound of delivery and trash trucks. If we were in the subway, the first train always gave a blast as it arrived at the station.

Sunshine and I ate reasonably well the first month or so on the streets. After that, I used my money for one good meal every other day for myself. She got a can of dog food each day, along with whatever she and I could find to eat on the street The thought of eating someone's leftovers used to be disgusting; now, it was only a matter of "it looks decent enough for me to eat." Sunshine never objected to any discarded food. Her palate and constitution were much more tolerant than mine.

Trying to conserve my savings, I finally ventured to become a beggar my second month on the street. On that morning the bells at Park Street Church chimed nine as I began my new way of life.

Sitting outside the subway station on the ground I experienced a feeling I never had before. So many times I'd seen men and, yes, on occasion women begging at this very spot. I had never known until now what they felt. Sadness, despair, a rush of guilt, and shame filled my whole soul.

That very first time putting my hand out and begging was so hard. I felt my eyes fill up; my heart was racing. I couldn't believe how hard this all was. Sunshine sat next to me; she leaned in extra hard to give me comfort and courage. It was as if she could feel all my emotions. She sighed heavily and rested her chin on my leg as if to say, "It will be okay, I am here with you."

Looking into each person's eyes passing by, I finally got up the courage to put out my hand. My voice cracked. "Can you please help me out, anything?" The rush of people that went by made me feel invisible. Tears ran down my face for no apparent reason other than I couldn't believe where I was.

"Please, can you spare a dime?"

After a few minutes I'd settled in, gathered myself, and began to feel a connection to the ground. Looking up would now be the norm; my outstretched arms would be my lifeline. It was then ten, and the bells tolled again.

Time slowly went on. Sunshine and I found benches on the Common or the Public Garden to sleep on during the good weather. The inclement weather drove us underground to the subway when we needed a warm safe place to hide and sleep.

Our morning or nighttime strolls took us all around, sometimes to the South End or Beacon Hill. We would visit the local missions for lunch, dinner, or just for a cup of coffee. When you're homeless, you found your brothers all around. Some of them were helpful; some tried to steal from you.

Each man I met on the street had a story of his life going wrong. In most of their stories, I realized that they thought they were not to blame; life, the family, jobs were the culprit. Yet it never seemed they had any culpability in their decline.

Their names became a blur after a time. The Jims, Johns, Harrys or Steves mattered not. You could place any name on any man; it did not seem to much matter. We were all nameless souls who survived, or didn't, on the streets.

We would, for the most part, keep in contact with one another. There was always the line, "Hey, have you seen Bob around? He hasn't been around much lately." Men would drift away, some would die, and others would end up in the drunk tank or go mad. Who knows, maybe a few made it back to the land of the living. Homeless life was becoming harder for me to handle; my mind, I felt, was going crazy. Sadness stayed with me longer each day. I became more anxious and easily upset. If not for Sunshine I would not know how to face each day.

During our walks I always tried to bring in some humor for me and Sunshine. What the hell else could I do? We found it a treat to walk by the TV appliance stores. Sunshine and I would sit across the street and watch the afternoon soap operas. Of course, we couldn't hear any of the dialogue, but nevertheless it was entertainment. Sometimes I played out what was happening, especially when the actors got animated on screen.

"What, you don't love me anymore, you're in love with Ashley?"

Tears fall. "Yes, I love her, but I love you as well!"

Sunshine looked at me as if I was asking her these questions; I had a big belly laugh at all this nonsense.

Chapter 11

SLEEPING

The fall season had come, the nights were longer, and time spent sleeping on the bench turned out to be much harder. My suitcase was lighter than when I left my last apartment. My suits were long gone, replaced by sweaters, sweatshirts, socks, gloves. Pretty much any form of clothing I could layer.

There were a few nights during the month that Sunshine and I were awakened by the police, depending on where we were sleeping. The sound of the nightstick cracking on the bench always startled me. Sunshine and I leapt up.

"Move along, you know you can't be here!" The voice of a policeman was very distinctive. "Come on, gather your stuff and get going."

"Yes, sir." I never argued or gave them a reason to arrest me. Sometimes I would have loved to, but where would Sunshine end up? On those occasions, we found an alleyway or doorway behind a building. Those locations were great to take cover from the wind and rain, but you had to deal with being in an area where rats run the show.

Sometimes Sunshine and I looked for an unlocked car to sleep in. Most people locked their vehicles, but we could always find one to sleep in if we tried hard enough. We saved this adventure for the cold, snowy, and rainy nights when we didn't get to the subway in time to find shelter.

Most nights during the week, if a car was parked, it was there for the night. Boston's working and blue bloods cherished their parking spot just as much as a good night's sleep.

This particular night I'd waited too long to get into the subway. After a long walk jiggling all the car door handles, we ended up on Beacon Hill. It was just after one, the church bells had finished. I could tell this was going to be an awful night to be outside. Sunshine and I found this beautiful '53 Chevy, and to my surprise it was unlocked.

Sunshine jumped up to the car's floor from the sidewalk. In a second, she had curled up and was heading to sleep. As luck would have it, there was a blanket in the back seat. "Thank you, God," I whispered to the sky. As the heavy rain began to beat on the car's window, I pulled the blanket over me and slept as if I was asleep in the arms of Jesus.

I cannot remember when I felt so safe and relaxed. The hard, loud rain made it easy to find rest and drift away. I thought I was only out for a few minutes when suddenly, we were awakened by the sounds of daybreak. This time it was not nature sounds or subway trains, but the sounds of people chattering outside.

I opened my eyes, not having a clue as to where I was. Then there was a banging on the window, and a loud voice telling me to unlock the door and come out. Sunshine sat up. She, too, had enjoyed a night of very restful sleep.

Pulling off the blanket, I sat up and pulled up the lock button as the back door was flung open.

"Come on, get out of there right now."

I could tell it was Boston's finest. "Yes, sir," I shouted. Grabbing my belongings and Sunshine's leash, we stepped onto the sidewalk to a small group of onlookers and two police cars, along with a paddy wagon. The crowd of folks whispered to each other as one of the police officers told me to get up against the vehicle. Another officer took Sunshine's leash from my hand.

The first police officer asked, "Now, what were you doing in this car? Trying to steal it, I suspect?"

"No, officer, I was not. You see, it was pouring rain last night. My dog and I were looking for cover from the rain, and we fell asleep. I'm sorry. We meant no harm." The voices of the crowd were not helping my case. Some of the men spoke up loudly with harsh words to have me arrested, while the lady's whispers of disdain and shame came my way. I had heard these words all too often about what I am. But this morning all the slings and arrows cut deep into my heart.

"Let's move along, folks," another officer shouted. Just then, the cuffs went on my wrists. The officer who had roused me was now escorting me to the wagon.

I pleaded, "Sir, please, we did not break anything, the door was unlocked. Wait, what is to happen to my dog? Where will she go?"

"Come on, let's go."

I was led into the back of the wagon. The two heavy back doors closed, and the door locked. As I looked out the small glass window reinforced with wire, I could see the officers laughing a bit, I assumed at my plight.

Sunshine sat very submissively—it was as if she knew

to behave. One of the policemen held onto her rope. I smiled at her as we slowly drove away to the station.

It should have been a short ride to District One, just a few blocks away. Less than five minutes, I figured. The men in blue took the long way back to the station, though. Every left and right turn was a sharp one, which caused me to nearly fall over onto the floor. Trying to sit on a wooden bench with my hands in cuffs behind my back made it impossible to stay upright. The worst was the quick stops and starts. I bounced off the back door when they hit the gas and slid forward when they braked hard. I could hear the officers laugh from the front of the cab. They needed to have fun with the prisoner, I guessed.

I was determined to be upright when the back door opened. To the men in blues' chagrin, I was.

"Okay, let's go, come on." I stepped down from the wagon and walked into the station. I kept my mouth shut for a time.

"We got another drunk vagrant here," the officer announced loudly for all to hear. "He was, get this, sleeping up on Beacon Hill in the mayor's sister's car, can you beat that." They all chuckled loudly at my situation.

I was scared. I felt my stomach flip, almost to the point of being sick. *I can't believe this is really happing.* I'd never been in trouble, not even when I was in the Marines—never a fight, not a demerit. I took pride, the little I had left, in following the rules.

The desk sergeant looked down at me from his enormous wooden front desk and, in a low, heavy Irish tone, said to me, "You picked the wrong car to be in, my friend. Most times, my boys let you fellas out around the corner with a warning. That will not happen today; we have too many issues to let this slide. Let us get all your information." The sergeant asked for my license or ID, of which I had none.

"Okay, do you have any documents telling us who you may be?" he asked.

"Sorry, Officer, all I have is my Warren Bank savings book. It has my name and where I used to live."

The officer looked it over, then filled out more lines on the forms without asking many more questions.

"Okay, Mac, take his prints and put him in the tank for a bit." The arresting officer, Mac, grabbed my arms and led me to the holding area.

Metal keys opened the squeaky iron cell door. The officer took off the cuffs and pushed me into the cell. A few other guys were sitting on the benches, some asleep, others coming out of a stupor.

As the door closed, I asked the officer. "Sir, what about my dog? What happens to her? Can you let me know what I need to do to get out and retrieve her?"

"You will get a chance to make a call in a few minutes, once we finish processing you."

I stood in silence for a moment. What had happened? I found an empty bench to sit on, the smell of stale booze, body odor, and vomit circling around me. This odor made an interesting concoction of fragrances, nothing that anyone would like to be around for any length of time.

As I racked my brain over where they would take Sunshine, I didn't realize that I was talking out loud. Then, finally, one guy, older, beaten up by life, spoke to me.

"You got a dog, hey?"

I looked in his direction and said, "Yes." Looking closer at his tanned worn-out leather face, I guessed that he must have had a life on the seas. He grinned, his head moving side to side. It was apparent that he was still deep in his cups.

"Dogs, dogs, they kill all the dogs. We're all dogs, they will kill us all, two-legged or four," he shouted and laughed.

I got up and sat on the dirty floor, away from this drunk. Sitting alone, I noticed that the whole area was quiet. I posed a question to all who could hear.

"When do we get out of here?" No one answered. I shouted a little louder this time. "When do we get out of here!"

Another voice in the cell said, "Not till Monday. We is all here for the weekend, so shut up and go to sleep."

Monday? I cannot wait till Monday; what will happen to Sunshine if no one claims her? But of course, I already knew the answer to that question. She would be put down.

Chapter *12*

COURTS

My housing, thanks to the Commonwealth, was dreadful at best. All of us were moved into smaller cells from the holding tank. Some of the men had jail uniforms, a grey one-piece jumpsuit. Some of us stayed in our civies. Unfortunately for me, it appears that the City of Boston had run out of clean jumpsuits. Oh well; I was happy to stay in my garb.

The food was awful, with a piece of stale Sunbeam white bread and tomato soup for lunch. Dinner was not much better, just some sort of meat, lumpy potatoes, and undercooked green beans. On the other hand, the coffee was not too bad.

This was by far the most extended weekend in my life. Not since I was in the Pacific had I felt such dread of what the next moment would be. At times I had work to calm myself down—breathing became difficult, and I was sweating. My cellmate had wanted to call for the jail doctor. I convinced him that I was okay, but my mind wandered all weekend to places, dark places, from my time in the war.

Saturday went to Sunday, and Monday morning would bring my freedom, I hoped.

That Monday, men left the cells every twenty minutes or so, one by one, and didn't return. I took comfort that I would hopefully be in that same situation. Closing my eyes, all I could do was smile and think of Sunshine.

Just then, a voice shouted, "Last man in the cell, come on, it's time to see the judge."

I leaped up, dusted myself off, then walked briskly with the guard—in new shackles—to the courtroom. The judge looked down at me as my court-appointed lawyer sidled up to me.

"Hi, I'm Steve Powers. I'm here to get you out today. I read the police report. It looks okay; you simply picked the wrong car to sleep in. They want to charge you with the theft of an automobile."

My heart fell through the floor when I heard what the charges were.

"Mr. Powers, all I did was fall asleep in a car. Trespassing yes, but not stealing a car. I was taking cover from the storm. I've never stolen a car. Me and my dog, we were both just sleeping." As I pled my case to my lawyer my voice grew a bit louder. My counsel was not listening to or looking at me. Instead, he was shuffling papers and scribbling notes on the margins of his yellow legal pad. I looked up at the court officers that flanked the judge's bench. Their folded arms dropped in unison, and they looked sternly at me. I knew I had to lower my voice or possibly be sent back to the cell to calm down.

"Mr. Powers, how does your client plead to the charge of theft of a vehicle?" the judge asked in a booming voice.

I stood in silence, in a fog, not sure that any of this was real as my legal rep and the judge went back and forth. Minutes had passed when the gavel went down, knocking me from the daze.

"I'm ... what just happened?" I asked.

"You're free to go. The court wants you to seek counseling for booze, possibly AA? You will need to document your meetings and give them to the court."

"But I was not drinking." I tried to protest this more, but my lawyer held up a hand.

"Let me explain: it does not matter if you were drunk or not. You want to fight this bogus charge, then stay in jail and hope for bail, or another court date. Or you can take this as a gift and move on. That is my advice to you. What do you want to do?"

"I want to get out and find my dog!" I said sternly.

"Good, then let's work on getting you released."

Before I left the courtroom to be processed, I thanked Attorney Powers for his help and for setting me straight. Just as I was being taken to the back of the courtroom, I asked my lawyer one last question.

"One more thing. Do you know where they put stray dogs?"

He looked confused at my question, almost as if it there was a joke coming.

"Yes," he replied after a moment, "there are two locations. One is in the South End, the Animal Rescue League of Boston. I think they have another site over in Jamaica Plain on Huntington Ave. I would try the South End on Chandler Street, I believe, first."

I thanked him again for everything he did for me. I know I could have asked the court officers or the police for such inane information, but I thought they would mess with me, maybe take me on another ride in the wagon for a cheap laugh. After all, I was a hardened criminal; a car thief, so the charges say. In fact, I was just a man with his dog looking to survive each day without harming anyone.

It took about an hour or so to be processed out. I had to sign many documents, with the promise to be good and come back to court in ninety days. I read none of the fine print. I could have been signing that I started WWI; it did not matter. I walked out of the court, a free man, to find the Animal Rescue League of Boston.

It was close to 11:30 when I got out of court. I rushed across the street to hail a cab.

"Quick as possible, I need to go to Chandler Street, the Animal Rescue League."

"Okay, bud." The driver put down the flag on the meter, and we were off.

As we raced over to find my girl, I looked out the window at the people going about their business. Hopefully, I would be back with Sunshine begging for money soon. It was a strange feeling to be in a cab. I could not remember the last time I had been in one. Thoughts of doom rushed through all corners of my mind. *What if Sunshine is dead? Who will be my companion? I cannot do homeless alone; it is just too hard.*

In less than ten minutes and one dollar and eighty-five cents later, we were at the animal rescue. I gave the driver two dollars and rushed out of the cab.

When I opened the doors to the shelter, I couldn't help but notice the smell. It was unique to dogs and cats, a concoction of fear and urine, along with Lysol cleaning solution and pet dander. Rushing up to the counter, I asked where my dog was. The young lady took out some papers for me to fill out.

"What type of dog do you own?" she asked.

"She is a mutt about medium size, a happy, wagging

girl. Her name is Sunshine." I rushed to fill out the paper-work. "Is she here?" I asked frantically.

"When was she brought in?" the lady asked.

"Ah, Friday afternoon sometime, I'm not sure when. The police would have brought her in."

"That may be a problem; we only keep strays for forty-eight to seventy-two hours, depending on when they arrive. We get so many dogs that it is hard to keep them all, especially if they have no tags or IDs. If no one claims them, we must, by law, put them down."

I could hear dogs barking in the back as the door from the reception area and the kennel opened and closed. My head spun with the thoughts that she had been put down. I hoped to hear her bark, then realized that she never barked.

"Can I possibly go and take a look and see if she is here?" I asked.

"Yes, of course, come this way." The lady smiled a convincing smile that all would be okay. I took her good feelings with me as I walked into the dog area.

The holding area for lost pets reminded me of a very large Quonset hut the Marines used to have. This one was larger than the huts I had been in, but had the same feeling—a cold, multi-use building. Large metal cages were stacked on top of each other in three rows. There had to be fifty or more just on this aisle alone. I looked carefully into each cage, scanning side to side for Sunshine.

The lady shouted to me over the barking, "So if you find her, we won't hear you if you shout it—you'll have to come back out front."

Nodding to the lady, I slowly walked the aisle, looking intently into each cage. I noticed that most of the dogs barked louder the closer you came; if you happen to stop by their cage, they stopped barking and their tails wagged like a whip. They all had sad eyes and huge smiles, and some even managed to put a paw through the cell. "Yup," I said quietly, "everyone wants to get out of their cage, whether you have two or four legs. It matters not when you're locked up."

Workers helped potential owners as they walked around the kennel looking for dogs that might be best suited for their forever homes. My heart raced with fear that Sunshine was already gone. Was she at a different location, or worse? Maybe someone else had claimed her. I could live with that, I thought.

Walking down the last aisle, I could see a few empty cages. What had happened to these dogs?

There was no sign of Sunshine, and my heart sank. I would grab a cab and go to the other shelter.

The loud barking in the background was deafening. Why did she not bark? If she had, I would have known her voice, her sound. In frustration I shouted out, "Sunshine, where are you, girl?" The dogs stopped barking for a moment, and the workers and clients looked at me.

I looked at everyone and sheepishly said, "Sorry, I'm just trying to find my dog."

No one paid me any mind; they all went back to barking or talking as I slowly walked around the hut one more time.

Up ahead, not more than three cages away, a wet brown nose came partly out from the cage. Could it be her? I rushed over, knelt down on the floor, and saw it was my Sunshine. She must have been hiding in the corner of the cage. I hadn't seen her when I passed by the first time. She wagged and wagged her tail, smacked her lips, and whimpered a hello to me. I stuck my fingers in the cage to touch her face. *Yes, my dear, you are just like me when I was the last to get called out of my cell.*

Sunshine wagged and danced a little as I looked into my friend's eyes. Most people would think I was crazy, but Sunshine and I had a bond; I wasn't sure how or why, but I understood that we were meant to be friends.

"Hello, anyone here? I found my dog, she's here," I shouted. Tears fell fast from my eyes; relief and joy filled my soul. Then, as I gathered myself, the lady from the shelter came over.

"I see you found your girl," she said, smiling at me. "Come with me and let us fill out these papers." I jumped up and told Sunshine I would be right back.

"You know, you're incredibly lucky that your dog is still here. You should have a license and a good collar for her. The dogs we get in that have no ID are usually the first to go, after seventy-two hours. You can see how we are over-the-top with canines."

The lady went on to tell me the troubles of the shelter. I pretended to listen, but all I could think about was getting out, getting free.

"Yes, I'm going to get all the correct paperwork and license tags for her," I assured the lady. I knew I was in for a sermon on what I should do and how to take care of my dog. I would listen a bit more, take the documents, put them with my release papers, and most likely lose all of them.

Filling out the paperwork, I put in my old address and where I once lived and worked. I knew that if I said I was homeless, Sunshine would not be going with me. It took about twenty minutes to get her free. They were happy to have another dog reunited with its owner, and I was over the moon to have her with me.

Skipping, dancing, running, we did all those activities along with many sloppy kisses just outside the dog prison. We had many stories to tell each other. "Was your food any good? How were the sleeping arrangements, and your cellmates? Did they snore?" Sunshine smiled and rolled around on the ground for a much-needed belly rub.

It was time to celebrate our freedom. I had a few dollars left in the Warren Bank, which was only a dozen or so blocks away at Tremont and Lagrange Street. The walk would do us both good. We both needed to breathe free, clean air.

Chapter 13

FREEDOM

Walking along that day, I came to the realization that we all needed contact in the world. No one should be alone; we all needed a companion, and mine happened to have four legs.

I had cleaned up a bit inside, as the cons would say. Even a few days in the cage could change your mind about your freedom. A used but clean white shirt, new socks, and underwear filled out my wardrobe, thanks to the Suffolk County jail. They could not find brown khakis in my size, but that was okay; it felt good to be clean and have a fresh start.

Having a sawbuck in my pocket from my account at the Warren Bank, I felt flush. Sunshine and I walked around the corner to Jacob Wirth Restaurant. This fine establishment served the best German food around. It had been a Boston staple since 1844, or so the sign said. All I knew was that the leftovers in the trash out back had been delicious. I was sure eating from the menu would be ten times as good.

I tied Sunshine's leash, a new one thanks to the lady

at the rescue league, to the wrought-iron fence outside the restaurant. Then, after giving kisses to my dear friend, I went in for an order of bratwurst, coleslaw, and a fine piece of German chocolate cake.

Ahh, the pleasing smells of a German kitchen. It was my sense of smell that finally wiped away the aromas of my jail and Sunshine's. After finishing, I was out the door and over to the park near the Floating Hospital. Sunshine was very excited about this food. We sat down, relaxed and took a few breaths in and out, then we enjoyed our feast. The sun shone brightly on this side of the street. It all felt wonderful as the giant sidewalk clock in front of Jacob Wirth's gonged three.

Chapter

RATS, OR BACK TO THE JUNGLE

Often rats will find us. Those are the true enemy of all that live here on the streets. The bugs that crawl in your hair or on your body are nothing compared to vermin that rule the city at night.

I try to keep Sunshine close to me when we sleep. Sometimes she likes to be under the blanket, other times near me or partly on my legs. My jacket is always zipped up to the top no matter how warm it may be. I have a stocking hat and worn-out gloves, all protection from creepy crawlies as well as to keep my body heat from escaping. There are not too many nights in Boston when it's warm enough not to need a jacket or blanket. Before I call it a night, I pull out my old dirty pillow from my satchel to rest my weary head on.

There was one night that I will always remember. It must have been just after two in the morning when Sunshine and I were awoken by an unexpected heavy rainstorm. I always scanned the night sky before we took refuge. If there were heavy looking rain clouds, I never chanced being out. Those times, Sunshine and I headed to the train station early to hide,

We had found a good bench in the Public Garden. What I mean by a "good bench" is that the wood has a slight bend at the bottom, toward the bench's back. It curved wonderfully to support your back when you were sitting and was even better to curl into when you were sleeping. Unfortunately, some benches were just flat planks of wood, not particularly good for your back. Thankfully, the Public Garden trustees had bought better ones.

It had been a long, hard, emotional day for the two of us. Sunshine and I didn't usually bed down till eleven or so. That night was different: we had a good hot dinner in our bellies, had taken a slow stroll around the Common, and the lovely Garden made the night perfect. I told Sunshine all about my adventures. She would move her head side to side and pretend at times to be interested. Other times she washed her belly while I rambled on.

Sunshine sat up on the bench, curled into a ball, and wasted no time in falling asleep. I was still setting up my makeshift bed on the bench when I heard her snoring. The Park Street Church bells stuck ten as I lay my weary head onto my pillow. Looking up to the sky, I noticed the bulb in the streetlamp was out on the Common pathway. This gave us more cover so we would not be noticed.

Checking the sky then, it was clear and calm, no wind to speak of. Before I drifted off, I thanked God for all that I had. As I closed my eyes to sleep I gave Sunshine a hug.

A tremendously loud clap of thunder woke both of us. It was as if the clouds were right over us. My heart raced back to the war and the sounds of the ships' guns firing missiles over our position.

Sunshine jumped down from the bench and set to shaking the water off her coat. The quick downpour soaked the both of us. I gathered up everything as we both ran to the nearest building on Charles Street. It was far too early to start our day.

We darted back and forth to each side of Charles Street, looking to find the best place to sleep. The darkest and out-of-the-way location was always best. We finally settled in a doorway with a ten-foot indent before getting into the store. These indents, or horseshoe-shaped store fronts, were great for window shopping. Each side had a display of shoes, boots, or whatever the merchant was selling. This would serve as a perfect hideaway from the cops driving past, or anyone that may be walking by. Not that they would be in this storm. Watching the rain pelt the sidewalk from our dry vantage point, I again went back to the Pacific.

Soaking rains, blistering hot days, and humidity made your whole body drip constantly on the islands. You never felt dry—I think I felt the driest when I went for a swim in the Pacific Ocean. It took about two weeks for the base camp to construct a makeshift shower. All they had to use was the saltwater from the ocean due to the fact the fresh water was a precious commodity. For days or weeks, you would be in the same clothes. We all smelled terrible, even the enemy. After a short time, you forgot about vanity, especially shaving. Staying alive was the only goal. A bullet or a bite from a mosquito might be your demise.

I remembered one man from our unit went crazy. Most of us were a little unhinged from fighting, but this day was different. I cannot say that I knew George from Georgia very well. He was a tall, thin, strapping fellow, at least six feet eight inches tall. Most of the Marines in our unit were under six feet. That worked out very well, as we spent most of our time crouched down in holes that were man- or bomb-made. Although we'd gotten into a few conversations and had some laughs, it was hard for him to understand me, and I felt the same about him.

On this particular day the rain was heavy and constant. It had started before dawn and kept going till late in the day. All of us had hunkered down; we and the enemy were not going anywhere, just keeping watch on the line. We'd had a firefight with the Japs early in the morning. It was not much to speak of, really. Mortar rounds, some gunfire, and then it ceased as quickly as it began.

Suddenly, George stood up from the foxhole. He began to murmur at first, then started yelling, then screaming about not being able to stand up.

"No, no, I want to stand up!" he cried.

The Marines in his trench told him to shut up and tried to pull him back down. Then one shot echoed out, like a clap of thunder, and George was no more.

We all grew up fast seeing death all around us and inflicting the same on the enemy. How many of them went crazy like George, I wondered.

Back by the storefront, I quickly changed out of my pants, shirt, and socks. Opening my case, I grabbed my dry clothing. Hanging the wet articles on the store's doorknob, I hoped they would dry before I woke. Unfortunately, my blanket and pillow were soaked. Nevertheless, Sunshine and I both laid down on the ground, using my jacket as a blanket and the case as a pillow. Curling up in the fetal position, Sunshine and I held onto each other for warmth and to get dry. The sound of the hard rain lulled us asleep.

The feeling of waking up to something running on you was creepy and unnerving. The number of rats running over us made me scream. I yelled, cussed— Sunshine jumped up and started to chase the rodents. It seemed that they were surprised to find us here.

One rat was on his way up the bottom of my pant leg. I jumped and shook him out before he bit me. One could only assume they were all on the run, like us. They too had ducked into this area to hide.

Some went scattering under the door where my clothing was hanging, while others ran back and forth in a confused state. More ran out onto the sidewalk hugging the building and searching for an opening to disappear into. I looked over to see how Sunshine was. To my surprise, she had caught one of the rats. Two shakes and a crunch of her jaw, and the rat was no more.

This was disgusting. I'd had rats around me before. Once in a great while, they might run over my body as I slept. One time, a rat had bitten my right hand when I slept in a trench in the Pacific. Thankfully, I'd gone to the medic for shots. That was why sleeping up off the street on a bench was so important.

I shuddered, then yelled to scare off the remaining critters in our area. Sleep was done for tonight. Looking out onto the street, the rain had slowed a bit. I gathered up the wet clothing and draped it over my case. Sunshine was done with her late-night snack. We moved on down Charles Street, slowly heading to Cambridge Street.

Chapter 15

QUIET

A slow walk in the early morning between three and four is blissful. The birds are still asleep, and a streetlight at each corner and a few lights in the buildings are all that the city requires to be lit. One can hear the quiet; it is so loud, so empty, and yet so very peaceful. When the only sound is my footsteps, it's as if God is setting the table for a new day.

There are nights when sleeping in a phone booth is the best option. As crazy as that sounds, Sunshine and I enjoy a change of pace. The trick to sleeping in a phone booth is that you must find the ones with a seat in them. Most of the phone booths now are only for standing and talking, but Sunshine and I still know where there are a few seats remaining.

Placing my case on the floor, I close the bi-fold doors, which in turn signals the light to come on. I stand on the seat, loosen the glass shade, unscrew the bulb, and replace the shade. I then stuff newspapers all around the bottom of the booth to keep out the possibility of vermin. Sunshine curls up under the seat as I rest my body against the booth's glass wall. Before I fall asleep, I try my luck where the coins drop out. None tonight. Oh well, that is okay. It is not comfortable to sleep sitting up, but it is a perfect place to stay warm and out of the elements.

In the morning, I do everything in reverse. It's as if we were never there.

Another day begins as I watch all the well-dressed men and women move up and down the sidewalk. They are heading to their offices to start a day's work. The men are dressed smartly in suits, covered up by warm overcoats, hats, and gloves to complete the ensemble. The ladies are in the newest fashionable dresses, with cute hats, gloves, and high-heeled shoes. Most of them are purposely oblivious to me and Sunshine.

I watch some of the people go by. The younger folks have a jump in their step; they want to get a leg-up in the world. They rush by the masses, darting in and out, trying to get to wherever they are going just a second quicker. Middle-aged people are resigned to a more comfortable "I will get there when I get there" walk. They look confident. The senior workers are in the back of the pack, often looking around, stopping for a moment to look at scenery. Maybe they pause to have another cigarette before the day at the office begins. They are in no rush to be anywhere, especially work. Some look to be hopeful that today is their last day working.

"Hey buddy, why don't you get a job? Stop hanging out here, you bum." I look over to my right side, and I see a man holding a broom. I'm sitting too close to his store.

My head goes down to my chest for a second. I pause for another insult to be flung my way. Then I begin to gather up my belongings, stand up, and grab Sunshine's leash.

"I told you people, don't hang around here. I will call the police next time."

His words fade away as we walk down Tremont Street A few people look and point at us. I'm sure we will end up a story at their water cooler this morning. Sunshine and I slowly make our way, walking in the opposite direction to the masses.

Moving around is a constant. Everyone, and I mean everyone, does not wish to have you anywhere near their place of business. The neutral turf on the Common is a spot where we are less likely to get hassled.

Chapter *16*

BREAKFAST

"No need to rush, girl; we have no place to be." I pat her head. Sunshine and I will head to the dumpsters in the alleys for our breakfast again.

Walking halfway down the alley, we find the metal barrels filled with last night's dinners. Another trick to living on the street is to try to know the trash man's route; if I am correct, we can partake in the restaurant's left-over dinners. Taking off all the lid containers and placing them down quietly beside each bin, I survey the second-hand bounty as I go through each compartment. I find pieces of bread lying on top of hard spaghetti. Sunshine smells the barrels that she wants. I reach in and pull out what's left from a steak dinner. She loves it. Grabbing what looked like somewhat clean bread, I begin to eat what is edible. What's left I stick into my right jacket pocket for Sunshine.

"Hey, you, what are you doing?" Words Sunshine and I hear often.

Sunshine and I stop, look left, and see a lady standing alone in the middle of the alley.

"Why, how, why are you eating out of rubbish barrels?" she says in an irritated voice. "Come away from there."

Sunshine pauses, tilts her head, and walks toward her. "Hello, sorry, we meant no harm." I pull gently on the leash.

I explain slowly and in a soft voice that we are hungry, and, well, having no money will lead you to wherever you can find food. I place the lids back on the barrels, snapping them shut. I like to keep the goods from spoiling or the vermin getting in. I might, after all, be back here later. Or we might not. The lady has a very disapproving look.

"We will be on our way."

"Hold on, not so fast," she says in a stern voice. "I take it that you and your four-legged friend have not had breakfast yet?"

"Yes, ma'am." I tip my hat. "You would be one hundred percent correct. I have been bumming money on the streets this morning, and well, I haven't had a very prosperous day so far."

The lady laughs a bit and says, "Yes, well, I can believe that. But of course, no one should be eating out of the garbage. You know better than that. Why aren't you at the mission this morning?"

"You're right. It's just some days we don't feel like eating bad food and watered-down coffee. Besides, I cannot take my dog inside." I went on a bit more, telling her some of our daily struggles when she interrupted me.

"Wait here; I'll be right back," she said firmly.

I am always a bit cautious when folks say that. It sometimes means that Boston's finest is on their way. But I have a good feeling about the lady.

It takes less than five minutes for her to come back out.

"Here you go," she says, handing me a paper bag full of food and a hot cup of coffee. "This should hold you both for the morning and maybe get you through to dinner."

"Wow, thank you so much; this is very kind of you." I smile bigger at the lady, tip my hat again, and wish her the absolute best day.

"Yes, well, see that you don't eat out of the trash anymore. You could get sick, and then where would your dog be."

A little scolding from someone who cares is a good thing. She's right. What if I were to get sick and must be in the hospital. Her stern warning will stay with me.

Sunshine and I begin walking out of the alley. I haven't gone more than a few steps, but when I turn back, the lady is gone.

"Angels, Sunshine. Angels, they are everywhere. Especially when we least expect them," I shout loud for the alley to hear. The Arch Street Church bells chime ten.

Chapter 17

CHURCH/FR. MIKE

In good or bad economic times, many churches reach out to help those that need it the most. These are places of good people not only preaching the word of God but helping anyone when needed. Church is a refuge, a safe haven to take a break. A place where we are not judged, spat upon, and cast away; rather a place where we are welcomed with a smile and a kind word.

We never convene in the chapel area, but downstairs in the basement where we can talk with friends we haven't seen in a while. Some of the churches offer a hot meal on different days. Some give out coffee and donuts. The trick is knowing what day it is and which place is open. Sunshine and I have a route we take each week; I am always keen on getting her some good food. As good as all this is, there are so many times when I don't want to be with anyone, just Sunshine and the street, and connect with the world again.

One day at church I met one of the kindest men I've had the privilege to know. He was a man of true faith. You could see it in his eyes, his soul, hear it in his words.

It was a Sunday morning a few years back when I still had a job and a home. Getting up at 8:00 a.m. for church was a challenge. I went to Mass at St. Francis, better known as Arch Street—the "worker's parish" as it is referred to, because you can come to Mass all day long, weekdays, for a twenty-minute service. Lots of Boston's working Catholics drop in when they can. Sunday is different; you can enjoy the slower pace of an hour of celebration.

Dressing up in my "Sunday best," I was ready to hear the word of God. With the church being only a few blocks away, I wanted to be on time for Mass. The church was still full when I got there. Looking around, I found a seat in the rear pew. I then noticed a new priest come onto the alter.

He looked to be in his late twenties or early thirties. His hair was longer than most men's, and he wore the Franciscan traditional attire of brown robe tied with a white rope belt, finished off with sandals.

"Hello, my name is Father Mike. I wish to welcome you to Mass this Sunday."

I would come to know Father Mike over the years.

Chapter *18*

LOST

The world was once again changing. Rents were going up; my savings were depleted. I had used much of it to help my mom, as she helped me for years until she passed. Friends came and went.

Life seems to be so easy when times are good. Friends, lovers, good times, and laughter abound. I had many years of that life. Family gatherings on each holiday, cookouts and the occasional drop-in make life so great. Having no phone at home made it difficult to get ahold of me. Every second Saturday of the month I attempted to reach everyone I knew. A roll of dimes was more than enough to make connections. As time went on, though, I needed fewer and fewer coins.

Time, family, friends would move on if you didn't try and make contact. Once my job was gone and the prospects for finding another became slim, it was hard to see and share my life with everyone who had so much more. When I lost my last apartment, I pretty much gave up. I was thankful that my mom was not around to see where I ended up.

But I had one more shot at a job with the possibility of a new life before I gave in to my new, homeless state. That was my interview with Mr. Johnson, my last hope listed in the stark black newspaper of the Record American.

ONE LAST CHANCE

"I'm here to see Mr. Johnson," I said confidently to the receptionist.

The lovely young lady with shoulder-length brown hair and soft blue eyes looked up at me from her desk, smiled, and said nervously, "So, you're here for the job?"

"Yes, yes I am. I hope it has not been filled yet?" I said anxiously. It was only half past twelve. *There is no way they could have filled it yet.*

"Hold on." The young lady put her hand up to me as she called into the office.

"Mr. Johnson, there is a man out here in Reception. Yes, he says he wants to apply for the sales position. Could you come out here right away, please?"

Before she hung up the receiver, Mr. Johnson was opening his door. Standing in the doorway, I could barely see the room behind him. He looked to be a former football player, at least 6'2", broad shouldered, about mid-fifties.

"Can I help you?" he said, speaking louder than I expected.

"Hi, yes." I put out my hand to greet him. "My name is—"

Before I could go on, he was coming toward me, then behind me to open up the door leading to the street.

"Come on, let's go. I don't have time for you people." He gestured me to the door.

"I'm ... sir, what is the issue? I hoped to have an interview with your company today."

He hurried me, or better said gave me "the bum's rush" outside to the sidewalk. Holding the door partly opened, he said, "Look at yourself, you're a mess. Your suit is wrinkled, dirty." He pointed up and down at me. "You haven't shaved in days, and you smell like a brewery. Go get your life in order, man, look in the mirror. I don't have time for bums like you. Go on!"

The door slammed closed. My reflection shone back at me, and when I saw how disheveled I looked, I was shocked. I looked like a drunkard. Was I in a stupor where you didn't know where you were and what had happened? Blows to the head from Sonny Liston would not have felt as hard as this.

Moving on down the street, I walked without purpose, almost in slow motion, as the world around me kept moving. A few doors down, I once again looked in the store window at my reflection, peering closer. I could see how awful I really looked.

Thinking clearly for the first time in an exceptionally long time, I knew I could not go back to the bar. It was time to move on as the church bells chimed one.

Chapter *20*

IT'S OKAY

I hurried to Arch Street Church. Opening the doors, not pausing to bless myself with holy water, I rushed straight to the bathroom. Locking the door behind me, I peered closer into the mirror and for the first time in a long time, I saw I man I did not recognize. Tears flowed down my face. I cried aloud, uncontrollably as I fell to the bathroom floor. My heart pounded; it was so hard to catch my breath. All my pent-up emotions gushed out. I was weeping loudly, so loudly I had to place my hands over my mouth so as to not gather attention. More tears fell into my hands. I reached for the toilet paper to wipe my running nose. My whole body became limp.

I was so mad at myself, *and* God for not helping me. "How, God, did this happen?" I said in an angry voice as I looked up to the ceiling and shook my fist at him. It took a few minutes to calm down. I was weak, exhausted—I had no more tears to let out. I reached my hands on the porcelain sink and pulled myself up slowly to see myself in the mirror. I really was a mess, a drunk, a bum, a hobo. All the things everyone despises in a human being. My beard was unkempt, my hair a mess. Many months had passed since I'd had a cut.

I turned the faucet on, running the cold water over my hands to cleanse myself of myself. Putting my hands together, I splashed my face and hair, then took in a deep breath and slowly let it leave my body. Opening my eyes, I felt a burden lift from my soul. My heart was not as heavy. I tried to smile and to my delight, the person in the mirror did the same. Putting myself back together, I opened the door and walked into the back of the Chapel. A few churchgoers were filling in the pews. The next Mass would be in ten minutes or so.

There were not many folks in the Chapel. I felt safe enough to find the back pew and close my eyes. My chin fell to my chest. In the background I could hear the movement of people coming in. I was so tired I drifted off to sleep. I felt at peace.

I may have been out for a minute or so when I heard a man's voice ask me, "Can I help you? My name is Father Mike."

Opening my eyes, I saw Father Mike sitting next to me.

"I'm, well, yes, no, I don't know." I was all over the place. I was a bit embarrassed. *Did Father Mike hear my crying in the bathroom? Do I appear even worse than I thought I looked? Were the police called?*

"It's okay," Father Mike said in a kind, soft voice. "I can tell you are troubled. You can unburden yourself, my son."

I always enjoyed when Father Mike said Mass. The few times I made it to Sunday service, it made it all the better when he was at the altar.

It was hard to look at Father Mike, though. I was

embarrassed and relieved at the same time to be able to unburden myself. I studied the poor condition of my shoes as I told Father Mike a bit of my failures, and how I thought I would do more in this world. I asked him why God was punishing me, why was he judging me. Again, tears started to slowly well in my eyes. I finally got the courage to look at Father Mike. He seemed to understand everything without saying a word. His eyes, his soul—it was if I was looking into the eyes of Jesus. Again, I felt the burden of life's failures lift.

Father Mike smiled and said, "God loves you for all your shortcomings, and all the good you do. God knows your heart, he knows your struggles, and he is always with you. God does not punish those that have true hearts, but he challenges us all each day to make our way in the world." I nodded my head and said nothing. We sat for a minute in silence.

"Would you say a prayer with me?" Father Mike asked. I was never much of one for prayers, those were Mom's department. She had the Rosary, and that was good enough for the both of us. "Yes, Father," I said softly. Together we whispered three Hail Mary's and three Our Father's. Father Mike stood up from the pew and blessed me and said, "Remember you are never alone. God is always walking with you." I smiled and thanked him for spending time with me. I felt so relaxed. It was as if I could sleep for a week. The bells outside Arch Street chimed.

Chapter *21*

SUBWAYS

I try to get into the subway when I can. The warmth from being underground is lovely. Most nights and some winter days, this is my home. I sit on a wooden bench far away from the commuters. None of them go to find a seat at the end of the platform. They wish to have the best location for the doors to open on their journey onward. Fortunately for them and me, a train is never more than five minutes away.

I watch their anxious body language; I see the look of concern on their faces when the train or trolley is late. I often look down the tracks, listen for the faint sound of the oncoming train. When a train is less than thirty seconds out from the station, a white light on the wall goes out down on the tunnel. This light is below the lights that illuminate the tracks. Once you can see the light, you can really hear the train's low rumble coming down the tracks. It sounds like a monster. The screeching of the metal wheels on the metal tracks announces that it is getting closer. If you stand near the opening, you can feel the surge of air being pushed toward the platform.

The quick, short burst of the train's squealing brakes announces the arrival at this station. The metal beast comes slowly to a stop. In a whoosh, the doors magically open, and people of all shapes and sizes rush off as others run in, searching for the coveted seats. The train's doormen look out their windows, making sure all is safe, then close the doors. A buzzer sound tells the conductor to move onto the next station. I watch this play out time and time again.

As I sit and watch this dance repeat every five minutes, I sometimes lean over and whisper to Sunshine what she thinks of this man, this couple. "Do you think they are friends? Are they going on a date? What about that guy? He looks a bit sketchy. That group looks like they're late for a meeting. Some couples are dressed to the nines for a night on the town. What do you have to say about this, Sunshine?"

Sunshine is not impressed with my questions. I think she is asking me her own. Like, *when are we going for a walk, when are we eating?* We sit on the bench a while longer as I share my opinions. My mind spins to how I was once.

I fall back to a time during the war, the cold, hard reality of seeing death all around you. Would I be next, or my buddies? If I were to die, would it be quick and painless? Staring up into the night sky a world away, I knew there was laughter, music, family, friends out there. I was here, along with thousands of other Marines, keeping those sounds of life, the freedom of our way of life, safe from those who would take it away.

The shooting had stopped for a while; some men caught sleep when they could. I was on watch with others down the line. It was my second night on this tiny island,

and as scared as I was, I was excited as well. Sleep would not happen for a few hours.

A gentle breeze came and went all throughout my watch. It held hostage the smell of death. *Funny, death does not discriminate. It is a constant, harsh odor for both sides.*

I had just been in my first battle and survived. How many more would there be? I was sure there would be many. Rolling over for a moment to look at the whole night sky, I gave thanks to God, saying my "Our Fathers" and "Hail Mary's" under my breath. I swear I could hear other men down the line doing the same. Tears rolled down my face, making a small puddle on my neck. My world was at peace for a moment as I watched shooting stars dance across the sky. What a beautiful picture; it was so quiet.

I come back from my moment of the past when Sunshine whimpers. Another metal beast has arrived at the station. I felt sad all over when I went back to my time in the war. It opened old wounds, wounds that seemed to be deeper each time I visited.

Shaping myself up, I tell Sunshine the words she already knows. "We must be diligent. The Transit Police will sweep the platforms a couple of times during the day and night. We need to keep an eye peeled for them. Remember to bark when you see the officers, Sunshine— we will move onto the next trolley or train. In no time, we will be back to the warm station, only on the other side."

Sunshine plays along, moving her head side to side as if to say, "You have told me this many times. I understand, and by the way, I don't bark!"

Some nights we're lucky enough to sleep in the subway's bench. It all depends on who closes the station up. The last man out usually checks the bathroom and the platforms for any stragglers who missed the last train out. They are also on the lookout for us men who hide and seek a warm place in the cold winter to call home for the night. The station master, as he is called, must count the money, lock the change booth, and finally close the gates till the morning. I've come to know who is good at their job and who is not.

Come closing time I would walk to the end of the platform with Sunshine, step down the stairs, and hide either in the tunnel or just under the platform. There is ample room to hide in the latter. The only issue is the mice and rats that run constantly all around the train tracks. We never have to worry about the danger of "third rail." In every station they are on the far side of the tracks, so in case anyone fell onto the track they would not get fried by six-hundred volts. We sat in the dirt for a time waiting to hear the metal doors closing. The lights never went off in any of the stations, but that was okay. We would walk back up to the platform, find a bench, and settle in for the night.

If you went and hid down the tracks, there was always a chance another late train might come by. There are spaces every three feet down the whole length of the tunnel for workmen to walk into, so they can place their backs up against the wall and let the train rumble by. I was okay doing that, but Sunshine got so upset one night when we misjudged the last ride into Washington Street Station.

It was mid-February, and an extremely cold snap of weather sat in Boston. On these unforgiving days our begging was curtailed until the temps rose above twenty degrees. This time the snow, wind, and unrelenting cold kept Sunshine and I on the rails for three days. We rode the Blue to the Orange and finally to the Red Line all day long. It was a fun game to stand or sit, look out the windows of the fast- or slow-moving vehicle. We would watch people as they raced for the coveted seat. Some of them were given up with a tip of the hat to a lady. We noticed happy and stressed souls run on and off, some kind and others downright rude.

It was Sunshine's and my conclusion that the Red Line trains carried the most unhappy and stressed souls around. Maybe it was due in part to the fact that Harvard University had a stop, or that the other stops went into the financial district. We discussed this at great length as the passengers stared at us. What did we care? We were warm, happy, and having adventures.

My goal was Kendall Square Station in Cambridge. This is one of my favorites. The place is kept very clean, and it's far enough away from the end of the line to keep the cold air away. You never want to be at the end of the line at any station. Too many issues with rainwater running in or other bums walking down the tracks for shelter. Kendall was a good choice, or so I thought.

Stopping at Kendall Station, we got off and I checked the time on the large clock that hung near the exit. It showed the time to be 12:20; this was the last train heading to Ashmont Station. The train slowly left the station, gaining power and losing sound as the metal beast rolled down the tracks.

A few riders left the station as I pretended to tie my shoes. Sunshine and I walked down the well-lit tracks around the bend so the station master could not see us if he were to look down the tunnel.

"It will be just a few minutes, Sunshine, then we can have a bite to eat and find sleep," I told her. She sat next to my feet as I rested my back in one of the cut-outs. I would give it ten minutes and then we'd make our way back.

We were there for close to the ten-minute mark when the back of my head felt a vibration. I shrugged it off as nothing. Just then, I heard the screech of metal wheels on metal tracks and felt the air being pushed in our direction. My heart raced. *Oh my God, another train is coming our way.*

Sunshine wanted to run. I grabbed her leash and pulled it as close as I could to me. I looked down the tracks and knew we had no time to make it to the platform. Even if we were both to run, she might break away and hit the third rail. She yelped as I held her tight. The air rushed faster and faster toward us. My mind raced with thoughts of how stupid this was. I could not believe that I'd made the biggest mistake you could when in hiding in the tunnels: you never go backwards. You always want to walk down the tracks from where the train was, not the tracks where the train is coming into.

I pressed my body into the alcove, holding tighter to the leash than ever before. I put my right leg over Sunshine to shield her and keep her from darting out under the train. The sound of the metal on metal became deafening as the train rounded the bend where we were. The air rushed by and pressed us both closer to the wall. One car, then two, three, and finally the last one rolled by us. In less than twenty seconds it was over. Sunshine looked at me and I swear if she could talk, well let's have it said that her words would not have been kind.

A few deep breaths in and out for the both of us, and then we began a quick walk toward the station. The last train was slowly leaving the station—well I hoped it was. Sunshine and I hid under the platform for twenty minutes just to be sure.

Chapter 22

SIMPLE THINGS

My left hand holds onto the leather strap on the trolley car as it slowly rocks side to side; my right hand has Sunshine's rope. I hum a song, words from a distant time in my life, as I look over and see a mom and her young child watching me. She giggles at my singing, I smile back. Her mom whispers not to talk to me. The girl smiles and waves back at Sunshine.

The screech of the metal wheels on the metal tracks deafens my words. "This is Sunshine," I say. Pointing to her, I say a bit louder, "My dog is friendly. You can pat her if your mom says it's okay." The mom looks at me, then Sunshine, and lets her girl come over. The little girl gently pats on top of her head, and Sunshine bows a bit. The trolley goes around the bend, and the noise of metal on metal is a lot louder this time.

The trolley begins to slow as it approaches the station. The little girl goes back to her mom. Sunshine and I exit down the two stairs onto the platform. I tip my hat and wish them a day full of sunshine. The little girl smiles and then jumps onto the seat to wave bye to us. Not too much to make this man happy; a smile and the innocence of a child.

The morning rush hour is nearly over, with fewer people in and out of the station. I picked up a newspaper from the platform floor and read some of the stories out loud to Sunshine. She looks at me, unimpressed but attentive. "I feel the same way, girl," I say to her. Tucking the paper under my arm, we head out of the subway. It's time to do some begging.

We find a spot on the Boston Common, just outside of Park Street Station. The wind is not too harsh today—if it were, we would find a location where we didn't have the full force blowing on us, and where the sun would feel like a hug.

When you qualify to become a "bum, hobo, transient, down on your luck," any of those words that people call you, it gives you an identity in a club none of us wish to be included in. So many of us are drunks. Some of us are here for a short time, if they are lucky, and they get help they find a way to move on. Others, like me, have had a loss of jobs, family, and friends. We lose our apartments, move into a friend's home for a while, eventually find a flophouse, and finally are on the streets. After a while, you stop looking for work. You have been beaten down. You give up and become one with life on the street

The church bells chime: I count and find it to be ten o'clock. I raise my face up to the warm sun and take in the extra warmth on my body before beginning my panhandling.

This will be my second winter homeless.

Chapter 23

ANOTHER YEAR

A few coins find their way into my hat—not a bad take. I have enough for dinner and breakfast tomorrow. It's nearly midday, and time to take Sunshine for her walk.

I tend to stay at one location every day for the morning and evening rush hour. If the weather is inclement, I stay in the subway and wait for clearer skies. All the while I try to find a friendly face, that kind soul that will say, "Hi." Better still is a smile, but a greeting of any kind validates my existence.

I forgot for a time how wonderful it is to be called by your name—such a silly part of life I thought to myself. Married folks tend to use honey, sweetie, and other kind and not so kind vernaculars. Friends, workers, and family use your name all the time. Having a name, being called by your name, is so important. It hurts like a punch to the gut when you realize you have none of these people in your life. Your name no longer matters.

This hit home to me one afternoon when two friends who hadn't seen each other for some time met just a few feet from where I was begging. They hadn't noticed or cared that I was here.

"Steve, Steve Powers, is that you?" one man asked the other.

"Yes, hold on … Carl, wait, oh damn, I can't remember your last name."

"It's Peterson, Carl Peterson."

"Yes, that's right. How are you doing? You look swell."

"Thanks, so do you."

I had not looked up to see these gents talking—their smiles would be too much for me. The more I heard them talk, the more it felt like a knife in the back. So often, I listen to conversations and they make no difference to me. This encounter made me incredibly sad to hear. I was jealous, I guess. Either way, it was too hard to hear and see happiness this morning.

Both men walked away, their voices fading into the background. This silly thing of a name made me so sad. Getting myself together, I closed my eyes and tried to remember the last time anyone had called my name. Sadly, I had no idea; it had been many months, or even possibly more than a year. I call out to Sunshine a hundred times a day, and while sadly she does not know my name, she is a love.

One day I found the courage to make up a sign. The night before, Sunshine and I worked on what to print. Having a pencil in my pocket, I tore apart pieces of the bottom of a banana box I found in the alleyway.

"How about this, Sunshine, what do you think of this? My sign reads *Hello, my name is*—damn." I had to reach and tear off another, more significant section of the box. The letters would not fit on cleanly.

I tried coming up with a few other ways to greet passersby. Taking my pencil, using the side to draw, and shade in the letters … all-in-all, it looked bad.

It felt useless, too. Why would anyone care who I was, why would they want to know my name? I threw the cardboard away in disgust. *No one cares who I am, who I was.* I felt angry at myself for even trying to make this work.

I gave Sunshine an extra hug, and she seemed to understand. Turning her head to me and opening her mouth, she gave me a long, wet lick on the face. Despite her stinky breath, I was nonetheless thrilled and gave her a big kiss.

Sunshine always knows when I am having a bad day. You can't help but smile from the notion that, yes, someone knows me, someone cares for me, and to an extent someone loves me. She just has four legs, not two.

Early on in my journey of being on the street I realized that the most generous people, the kindest people in the world, are those who have the least. Each day that I beg, which is every day now, the folks that spare a few coins with me are those that look as if they are just a paycheck away from being with me on the streets.

Chapter 24

JOE & NEMO'S

It always feels good to stretch and get a long walk in. I untie Sunshine from her collar in a flash; she chases squirrels, picks up sticks, and dances around, having the most beautiful time on the Common. We walk all around the ancient grounds. It feels good not to be cold. My belly is rumbling, and I know Sunshine is hankering for some chow.

Calling over to Sunshine "Here, girl" along with a few tics of my tongue, she races to me, and I bend down to tie on her leash. We wait a second for the cars to pass, then head over to Joe & Nemo's for a couple of dogs for us both.

Those of you who are not familiar with Joe & Nemo's are missing out on some of the world's best hot dogs at the best prices. The trick I figured out with cafeterias and restaurants is to have an exhaust fan above a window or door to blow the smell of whatever it is that is cooking today. In the case of Joe & Nemo's, it is always boiled hot dogs. Yum!

I hitch Sunshine to the hydrant outside, give her a hug and kiss the top of her head. "You be good, no barking,"

I say out loud, so others will see that I haven't abandoned her. I make myself as presentable as possible, shake the dirt from my jacket and run my fingers through my hair. Smiling at my dear friend, I think about getting her some delicious food.

As I walk inside, the sweet scent of steamed hot dogs fills my sense of smell. When you're homeless, you find each day that you're here on earth is a blessing and, at times, a nightmare. Some of the simplest gifts in life are the smells.

I love the smell of fresh-cut grass on the Boston Common. The Common has wide open spaces to enjoy a leisurely stroll, and for some a pick-up game of baseball at one of the fields. Just across the street is the Public Garden. This area is a beautiful sight in the spring and summer when the flowers are in bloom. Walking through the Garden, you cannot help being happy smelling all the aromas from the different flowering plants.

A quick downburst of rain brings a unique scent when it hits the warm pavement. The best fragrance of all is food—especially the wonderful aroma of fresh coffee. I close my eyes and drink in these gifts each time I have enough money to savor this pleasure.

I notice a few middle-aged men and one older gent standing at the tall aluminum countertop facing the street The enormous broad, nearly floor-to-ceiling windows show off this fine establishment and the hungry working patrons. The men discuss sports or politics, I'm not sure, and I don't really listen—I can tell the older man, with dark sunglasses on, is listening to the other men talking.

I became more and more aware of my surroundings when I lost my last apartment. Being a street person means you better have a good sixth sense of the people around you. Some will surely look to do you harm if they catch you off your guard.

There are six people in line in front of me, and two men in what were once white uniforms are shouting out orders from behind the counter. As the line moves along, I look up at the lunch board for the prices. I know Sunshine and I can have two dogs each.

Making my way to the counter I ask, "Can I have four dogs, two plain, two all-around, please? Also, two cups of water."

I reach into my jacket pocket to find the coins to pay my bill.

"That'll be eighty cents," the man says.

Placing the coins on the counter, I see that I have only sixty cents. I hurry to search each pocket for the two dimes. I know I had enough money this morning. What happed to my coins, did they fall out of my pockets?

The man behind the counter looks down at me and with a dismissive voice says loudly, "Buddy, do you have enough? It's eighty cents!"

The worker is growing more impatient. Behind me the shuffle of shoes, work boots, and high heels become louder on the linoleum floor. Joe & Nemo's works on volume and getting people fed fast. People are getting annoyed with me. I hear the door opening and closing as more people come in. I scramble once again to search through each pocket, but don't find any of the money I thought I had.

"I'm, well, take back one of the dogs," I say quietly as I put my head down. I feel ashamed and embarrassed. It strikes me as odd to feel this way. When I beg, I no longer have any of these feelings. But when I am back in the world, buying food, being part of society, I feel what everyone else feels when they are put on the spot. I blink my eyes as the man sighs.

In a stern, louder voice he says, "You people. You know, we are running a business, not a charity. Go down to the mission if you want free food." His arms move about, pointing me to the door, making a scene for all to behold. He opens the bag, reaches in, and takes out one hot dog. It's one of the two plain ones for Sunshine.

"Hold on."

A voice from the corner counter behind me speaks up.

"I will pay for his food. Put it back in the bag." The older man who stood by himself speaks in a louder, more commanding voice.

The store goes quiet as he directs the worker to put the food back into the bag. I look over at him—he seems familiar somehow. I may have seen him a hundred times as he passed me on the streets. Then again, maybe I have never seen him before. I see hundreds of people each day, and most of them I don't remember.

He slowly makes his way to the counter, holds up the two dimes for the worker to see, and then tosses them onto the metal counter.

"We are square, right?" He looks sternly at the worker.

"Yes, sir," he says.

The coins seem to magically bounce and then slide from the metal counter into the wooden register below. My benefactor makes his way slowly to the door. Gathering my bag of food, I catch up to him as he's leaving. We both walk out the door and head over to Sunshine. She is whimpering a bit, excited; she knows the food is coming her way.

"Is that your dog? She sounds like she knows what is coming. What's her name?" my new friend asks.

"Yes, yes, it is. Her name is Sunshine." Wanting to thank the man I quickly say, "Mister, thank you, you did a kind thing."

He pays no attention to my thanks, almost as if they haven't happened.

"Now that's an excellent name for a dog. Sunshine, you say. Of course, you can't help but smile when you say Sunshine."

"Yes, she is my best and only friend in the world," I say happily.

The man looks up from patting Sunshine and mutters softly, "Hmm, is that a fact? Your dog is your best friend, you say."

Not wanting to take up too much of his time and kindness, I thank him again.

He places his soft hat firmly on his head, buttons up his coat, and asks, "Are you from Boston?"

A gust of wind blows down the road. Funny thing, I think to myself, *it feels warm, not cold as it should be.*

"Yes, proudly," I say. "Born and bred."

The man smiles. "So am I. Boston is a lovely place. Some people call it the Hub of the Universe." He laughs as he says that. "Be well and take care of yourself and your best friend, Sunshine."

He puts out his hand to shake mine. I haven't had anyone want to talk to me in an awfully long time, much less a handshake. I feel almost human for a moment.

I take his hand, thank him again, and we both smile at each other and walk away.

Sunshine wags and wags as I get closer; her tongue flaps out over her lips. I release the rope from the hydrant and in no time, we find an empty bench.

Sunshine sits patiently as I take out the goodies from

the brown paper bag. Her plain hot dogs are given to her first. In two bites, one dog and roll disappeared.

I've noticed that I have these moments of peace sometimes, harmony between me and the world when it seems all is good. I see clearly, hear better, feel peace all around me.

"Hold on, girl, not so fast. I don't want you getting sick." I open the cup of water and place it so she won't spill. Reaching in, I unwrap my dog. Unlike Sunshine, I savor every bit as some of the relish drips onto my pants. I have a few napkins, but then Sunshine cleans up my mess. Nevertheless, napkins always come in handy, for so many reasons.

I close my eyes and remember the sounds of the past. Laughter in the summer, friends, and family. My sadness and loneliness are kept at bay for a time.

Chapter 25

LEAVING THE SERVICE

I was fortunate that I found a job fast when I got out of the service in December of 1945. So many guys were pounding the pavement, knocking on doors for any kind of work. Some found day labor work, some worked in construction, others went back to school on the government's nickel. I went back as a "tin knocker," working in a factory fabricating sheet metal. I was happy for a time.

The world had changed in the three years I was gone. I had changed too, just like most of the other G.I.s that made it home. The world had so much promise. New starts, a new beginning, awaited us all.

Some of the best skills you learn in basic training are the ones that may save your life both in and out of war. Becoming a Marine prepares you for many facets of life— even becoming a bum.

It was great to be back in Boston. I went and stayed at the old apartment with Mom for a week until I found a place of my own. Going back to that life was not an option. It was wonderful in some ways to be back sleeping in my old bed, and having a homecooked meal was a treat, but I needed my own place and space.

The building and my apartment were not much to look at. I chuckled to myself that I had finally made it to the West End. The place came furnished with a full-sized bed and dresser, a kitchen table with three chairs, some utensils, pots and pans, along with mismatched plates, bowls and mugs for tea and coffee. A very worn-out couch, a sitting chair, and a scatter rug in the middle of the floor filled the parlor. The windows and curtains needed a good wash.

My bedroom had one window that only opened from the top. A curtain rod hung empty, waiting for the curtain to be installed. All I had for privacy was a once-white, now tar and nicotine Venetian blind. Upon a closer inspection of the items most were damaged, some worse than others, but they served their purpose. I would need some towels, sheets, and a clean blanket along with some food to make this my home.

Having lived without for so long, I was in no hurry to fill my life up with stuff just yet. I enjoyed the simple pleasure of having a clean bed instead of the ground in some foreign country. When our unit was not fighting, oh how wonderful it was to have leave. Fresh meals from the mess hall. Going to see a movie—any movie, it did not matter.

It was almost the weekend. Should I try to find my old friends, maybe take in a movie or dress up and head over to a local dance with the chance to meet a girl? So many options.

After finishing up my dinner, I located a phone booth across and down the street from my new home. Opening my wallet, I found a picture of my old sweetheart. On the back was her phone number. As I dropped the coins in, I remembered her smile. When I first got into the service, we'd had grand plans for us when I returned from the war.

I had already received my "Dear John" letter in late 1944. "Jody" took my girl, as the song says. We'd stayed in touch with long loving letters in the beginning, but as time passed the letters became less frequent. I gently rubbed my thumb over her picture, thinking of all the places she and I had been during the war.

The call went through. "Hello, this is Cathy," she said.

"Hello, it's . . . " Before I could speak my name, I paused. Her voice sounded soft, just as I remembered, and my heart sunk low. Oh, how I'd missed her.

Cathy perked up once she heard my voice. She asked questions about when I got back, where I was living. As she spoke, I remembered her soft skin, beautiful smile, and how she would put a dash of perfume behind her ears. I smiled as I listened, giving her short accounting of where I was and how I was doing. It felt like old times. We talked and talked only being interrupted every five minutes by the operator asking me to deposit another nickel.

She eventually and reluctantly told me she was recently married and would move to the suburbs in a month. A new start, she said as she laughed out loud. Best of all, she added with a shy chuckle, "I am having a baby in a few months." She was beaming, I could tell.

Our conversation wandered a bit longer. She wanted to know where I lived. Again, I dodged the question and gave even shorter answers to the others. Cathy seemed to be truly happy to hear from me.

Wishing her all the luck in the world, I promised to

keep in touch. It was a white lie; both of us knew that not to be true. Before our conversation ended, she said that she was sorry for breaking up with me. I started to say, "It's okay," but then we were disconnected; my last nickel had dropped. All I was left with were the dreams of what our life together could have been.

The squeak of the phone booth door seemed louder as I opened it than when it had closed. I hadn't noticed it when I went in. Rain was beginning to fall. I turned up the collar on my jacket and strolled back to my home.

Checking my mail, I found a letter that announced that our unit was having a reunion dinner on Saturday night at the local post. I assumed most of the guys would be attending. Unfortunately, some chose to put the past behind them as fast as possible—they would not participate in it. Those men said that life and all it had to offer was in the future, and the ugliness of war should not be celebrated. I partly agreed with the latter.

Chapter 26

MISS MAE

Sunshine makes a mild whimper, which causes me to open my eyes. Licking her lips, a big yawn and happy grin, she clearly wants the second dog. I oblige her with the rest of our feast. Finishing up, we gather our belongings and go on our way. It's getting colder, and yet the day is only half over. So much more time to kill before we find our place of rest tonight. I think for a minute to go to Filene's Basement to get a few pairs of clean socks, underwear, and maybe a shirt.

I love going to Filene's Basement, where you can buy a lot of clothing for not a lot of money. The Basement is a clothing store with products that did not sell upstairs in the Filenes store, and once moved downstairs it is discounted. If the merchandise stays on the rack for a more than a week it is then marked down again, so on it goes. You can find amazing bargains if what you're looking for in your size is there for a few weeks. Sometimes it is hit or miss on sizes and styles, but I'm never too concerned for style; hobo fits me well.

The best part of going into the Basement is, if you happen to know someone who works on the floor, they can help you find exactly what you're looking for. Lucky for me I found Miss Mae. Mae is a blessing in our lives.

I used to go into the clothing stores, the Basement included, and get the bums rush to leave. I admit that if I'd seen me coming in, I would want me out just as fast. One time on the streets, Mae and I got to talking about where she worked and the problem I had buying clothing. Mae had a disapproving look on her face. It was not going to be a problem for me ever again, as long as I came and found her.

It worked well for a couple of seasons' worth of clothing. She would find the marked, then marked down, and still better marked down clothing to make my money stretch. Best of all I would not be hassled. I had a helper, a guard of sorts to let me conduct my business.

Today, most everyone is dressed up for the office. Mae is no exception. She is a lady I would guess is in her early sixties or so, always very well dressed, her short grey hair never out of place, always with just the right amount of make-up on. Mae carries herself confidently. She walks with purpose, not too fast or slow. She knows to always leave enough time to get to wherever she's going without the look of being rushed.

I first met Mae when I started begging at Park and Tremont Street, just outside the T exit. If I remember correctly, she was one of the first people to be nice to me. It all began with a "hello" from her. I was surprised when she said it to me the first time. The norm in society is not to see and interact with bums on the street.

Most of the time when I make eye contact, he or she will always look away. Not with Mae; she greeted me first. I looked back at her and said, "Hello."

Mae stopped just a few feet away, looked back at me

and asked, "What is your dog's name?" I smiled and introduced her to Sunshine. Mae smiled and said, "Good morning, Miss Sunshine." I tipped my hat to her as she went on her way.

It took me about two weeks to get up the nerve to ask this nice lady her name. "Hello and good morning to you," I loudly exclaimed to Mae from further away than usual. This would give me a few more seconds to ask for her name.

"I don't mean to pry," I said, taking off my hat, "but would you mind if I asked your name? I feel silly each day saying hello to you as you know my name and Sunshine's."

She paused and stopped right in front of me. Looking through her wire rimmed glasses she squinted, smiled, and said, "Well yes, of course you can. My name is Mae, Miss Mae Fielding."

"Hello Miss Mae, it is truly my honor to know you." Mae smiled and dropped a few coins into my hat. "You have a good day, stay safe and God bless," Mae said, and was on her way.

Seeing Mae each morning on the street would be the highlight of my day. I would whisper into Sunshine's ear when Mae was coming down the street, "Miss Mae is coming." Sunshine would sit up pretty, licking her lips with the hope of a dog treat coming her way. Mae would stop and smile, ask how Sunshine and I we were doing this day. Smiling back, I would tip my hat and say, "Miss Mae, we are doing splendidly this fine morning."

She would smile in return. "That's wonderful." Then she'd reach into her purse for a dog treat and hand it gingerly to Sunshine. In a flash it was gone. Mae patted her head and smiled. "I've got a little something for you as well." Mae would often bake cookies and Irish breads, and anything she had was a treat for me. On the odd times she had no food she would open her purse to find her small change purse and hand me some coins.

"Miss Mae, thank you but no, I cannot take your money. Just you stopping and being nice to Sunshine and me is enough." I would try to be firm with her, but somehow her coins usually made it into my hat.

Sometimes a faint Irish brogue would appear when Mae spoke. She seemed to be a bit embarrassed when I smiled at her accent. "Thank you very much Miss Mae, you are always very kind with all that you do."

Mae smiled, looked at me and said, "You know that I pray for you both each night."

Smiling, I bowed my head for a second. "Thank you," I said, "that's the best thing you could do, is pray. I will put you in mine this night as well. Again, Sunshine and I thank you."

I watched as Miss Mae disappeared into the crowds of people heading up and down Park and Winter Streets. The church bell began to chime nine.

Chapter 27

FILENE'S BASEMENT

A few days have passed, and I have not seen Miss Mae. It gets me worried, as she is always walking by my spot around eight-thirty or eight forty-five give or take, depending on the trolleys. Maybe she is on vacation, maybe she is ill. My mind wanders so much during the day. I ask Sunshine, "Where do you think Miss Mae is? Sunshine misses Mae's treats for sure. The sad look on Sunshine's face tells me how she feels.

Today would be a good day to get some new clothing; socks perhaps, maybe a sweater. *Let's go and check Filene's Basement. Who knows, maybe we can find Mae.*

I always need someone to keep ahold of Sunshine while I shop. I cannot tie her up to a hydrant or a sign. I always fear that someone may take her. As luck would have it, I see Jack, another man barely holding onto life, walking around begging. Jack looks like he needs a drink, and this morning's take has left him short of cash. You can tell when a man is desperate by the way he begs. Sometimes it is the pain of hunger, but most times it is the shakes of needing alcohol.

Hoping he is coherent enough to help me this morning, I walk over to Jack and tell him my proposition. I will give him some money or get him some clothing if he promises to stay exactly where I tell him to be with Sunshine. Jack loves the idea of cash; I can trust Jack for the fifteen minutes I needed.

Making our way over to Washington and Winter streets, I kiss Sunshine, hand the rope leash to Jack, and tell him to stand over by the wall across the street next to the Jordan Marsh Store. Jack grins and heads over as I walk down the stairs to the Basement. From here you can smell the subway and hear the Red Line subway trains coming and going at the Washington Street stop. To the right is the entrance to the store; head down a bit more and you're on the trains.

The hustle and bustle on the inside are amazing. Women, hundreds of women are flocking like herons from one counter to the next, looking at the handmade signs above the large open bins that hold the merchandise in mass piles. Nothing is neatly stacked, everything is wrinkled. Upstairs is the neatly pressed, orderly area.

Wandering away from the ladies' section and keeping my eye out for Mae while trying to stay under the radar of the store detectives, I can't help but laugh and remember when I was a young boy, and my mom would bring me here on Saturday morning.

I have no idea how old I was, maybe seven or eight when I was dragged along like all the other children to buy back-to-school or whatever season it was clothing. Money was always tight in our family; we had to buy at the bargain rate whenever we could. The only good thing about doing this awful chore was the blueberry muffins we would get at Jordan Marsh afterward, a big treat.

I remember one day like it was yesterday. Mom was rummaging through the bins, which I had no interest in. I turned away to look at what might be on the other counters across the way when, just by chance, I saw a lady take off her dress. It dropped to the floor with the greatest of ease, and the lady stepped out of it and began to try on another article of clothing. I'd had no idea what ladies wore underneath their dresses. My eyes bulged out in amazement. I was embarrassed and confused. I had never seen this happen anywhere—was this how all the ladies shopped? My mom had never tried on clothing like that. Well, at least when I was with her.

To be fair, very few men were ever shopping in the Basement, even though they had a whole men's and kid's section. Wives and mothers bought the clothing for everyone, I guess.

I blink my way to the present and find the men's section. It's fun to remember simple, innocent times, but I have business to attend to now.

I find a bunch of white socks, a sweater, and a pair of gloves. The jacket I want is too much. This will have to do for now. Heading to the cashier, I can hear the snickers and remarks heading my way. I look through the ladies as best as I can, trying to find my friend Mae. Slowly the line moves, and eventually I place my articles on the counter while the cashier rings up my bill.

I have to ask. "Excuse me, I don't mean to be forward, but I'm looking for my friend Mae. She works here in the store, but I haven't seen her in a few days."

The lady ringing me up stops chomping on her gum, pops a bubble, looks at me and says, "Mae, you mean Mae Fielding?"

"Yes. She is older, in her sixties I think, grey hair, very sweet."

"Yes, that's her. She passed last week, a heart attack we were told." Another pop of the gum. "That'll be two dollars and eighty-five cents."

I can feel my eyes blinking really fast as the clothing is placed into the paper shopping bag. I pass over three dollars and wait for the change to hit my palm.

My happy feelings have vanished, my smile is gone. Another person, another kind person has left my life. Walking slowly up the stairs to find Sunshine, the cold air hits my face like a slap. Sunshine comes running over once she sees me. Jack let go of the leash, but thankfully no cars were driving by.

"Here you go, Jack." I gave him a bunch of change from my pocket. I'm not sure how much it was but Jack took off pretty fast—heading for a bottle, I guess.

Chapter 28

WALKING

A long, slow walk on Commonwealth Ave to Kenmore Square, then over to Fenway Park, would be a nice treat. Walking through the Common, then the Public Garden, we slowly stroll onto Commonwealth Mall. Thankfully, there are benches to pause at when needed. I admire the Boston brownstones—the architecture is beautiful. Each home is five stories tall, attached to another with huge windows showing off grand staircases and chandeliers. I wonder how it is to live such a life.

"What is going on in their lives today?" I shout out to Sunshine.

I turn my head down and ask, "What do you think, Sunshine, would you like to live in one of these beautiful homes?" She smiles, wags her tail, and keeps on walking. Boston at night, especially in the winter, has a beautiful quiet. My hearing is not what it used to be, and having Sunshine with me gives me a good early warning just in case someone is around us that may wish to do me harm.

It takes about an hour or so to make it to our destination. Sunshine pauses on her own and sits at the corner of Brookline Ave and Lansdowne Street. I think it funny that she knows where we are. She looks up at me and then toward Fenway Park.

I smile at her and say," Yes, this is the home of the Boston Red Sox." Many a night I told her bedtime stories of Babe Ruth and Ted Williams and the wonder of Fenway. "Yes, Sunshine, you are correct. We are here. Although we could walk another mile down the street to Braves Field." Sunshine stands up, wags her tail, and gently pulls me toward the wall.

I marvel at the giant green wall in the city of red brick buildings. We walk down toward the "green monster." It looks enormous the closer we get. Sitting down at the wall base, I press my back and feel the sounds of games once played. I can smell the grass and remember how I felt as I walked up the walkway and saw the manicured infield grass. The players were warming up, some hitting from the batting cage, others running, and a few playing catch on the side near the first base line. All the players were smartly dressed in the clean white uniforms ready to play a game.

I take another deep breath in and out, close my eyes and remember how time stands still when you're at a ballpark.

I ask Sunshine, "Will 'Teddy Ball Game, The Kid' hit 388 this year?" He is nearly forty. What an outstanding baseball career he has had, plus two stints in the service. I compare his life to mine and see that God gives gifts and blessings to some more than others. Sunshine curls up onto my lap. I pat her.

"Listen, watch," I whisper into her ears and point to the imaginary home plate. "*Snap* the crack of the bat, *roar* of the crowd, and I see the baseball fly out of the Park and onto the street—another home run for the greatest hitter of all time." Sunshine looks confused as my story trails off.

The streets around Fenway are deserted. Like all of us, they are waiting for spring and summer when this area comes alive with fans. Dads will bring their sons to the park to see the boys play a game—one of the best games around. It's a rite of passage for every boy.

"Okay, girl, let's get a move on."

We stroll around the whole outside of the park, ending up on Jersey Street, in front of the Boston Red Sox office. It's just after seven in the evening, the far-away church bells chime in. Pausing to rest on the brick steps of Fenway Park, I shuffle my gear around from one shoulder to the next when the front door of the Park opened. A tall man walks right by me down the steps briskly to the curb.

"Hello," he says, looking back in my direction.

I push away from the building to catch a better look at the man. He looked familiar as he passed me. Well dressed; his smart-looking suit was easy to see due to his brown overcoat being open, but a soft hat concealed part of his face.

"Hello to you," I say back. Trying to look taller, I stiffen my spine. The man goes to the edge of the curb, then onto Jersey Street. He scans up and down, looking for what I assume is a cab.

Turning back to me, he asks, "You did not happen to see a car pull over and then leave by any chance, did you?"

"No, can't say that I have. I've only been here for a few minutes," I say.

"That's okay, sorry to bother you." He looks annoyed that his ride may have left without him. "So, say is that your dog? She is a beauty." Sunshine sits up, wagging and smiling—Sunshine knows kind people right away. She has a sense not to go over to someone that may be dangerous.

The man, whom I now recognize as Ted Williams, kneels and calls my dog over.

I watch him as he plays with her for a while. I smile and chuckle to myself that there's no doubt in my mind he could have made her the first dog to play in baseball. Ted stands up and does a quick assessment of me.

"How are you doing?" he asks.

He can clearly tell I'm on the streets. I can't lie to him. The man who can tell a fastball from a slider by the ball's rotation coming out of the pitcher's hand in less than two seconds would surely see a lie coming.

"I'm tolerable ... I mean, I am doing okay." However, he can clearly tell I'm a bit starstruck.

"You are?" he asks.

I want to divert from my condition. My mind goes back to when I was on leave.

"I once saw you play ball." How silly is that statement? Thousands of people have seen him play. I can tell he thought it was here or at some other ballpark.

"It was over in Pearl in '45, just after the war was over," I hurry to finish.

"You were in. What branch?"

"The Second Marines," I answer proudly. "I was at Tarawa. I made it onto the second wave, landing at the north part of the tiny island. It was a long three months to secure that piece of sand in the middle of nowhere." I go on a bit more, telling my story as I look at Ted.

He listens intently to my accounting as he plays with Sunshine.

Ted eventually speaks up. "I think they, the Japs, called that place Emperor's Island. Lots of wasted lives on both sides for what turned out to be not much strategic value. I may have even landed there once, not sure; I was all over the place. After a while, one airstrip on those islands all looks the same." Ted goes on a little more about his missions.

"Those were some hellish times, weren't they?" Ted asks in a way understood by those who have been in battle.

"Yes, sir, they sure were."

Ted looks up and down the street for his ride. We don't have much more to say. We both seem to be feeling a bit awkward.

"Hey, Um ... Can I give you a few bucks?" Ted reaches into his wallet.

"Thank you, Ted, sir, but I don't think that would work for me. I think spending a few minutes with you is worth more than money."

Ted has a wide smile. I ask him, "Why are you here and not in Florida?"

"Well, to tell you the truth, I just signed another year with the Sox, and for good money." As soon as those words are in the air, I can see that he wishes he could take them back; he looks a bit embarrassed. Ted again scans up and down for his ride, which is still not here.

"That's great, good for you. You deserve all and then some," I say confidently.

"Well, who knows how many more years I've got playing this game? It would be great to win the God-forsaken World Series before I retire. Maybe this is the year, what do you think?"

I smile at him as his ride pulls up to the curb. He reaches down to pat Sunshine one more time.

"You and Sunshine take care." Ted pauses, looks at me, and says, "Thank you for keeping that airstrip safe for all those other pilots, and especially me." I stand tall, smartly clap my shoes together, and salute Ted. He smiles and salutes back and says in a stern military voice, "Carry on, young man."

As he turns and walks to the car, I yell out onto the empty street, "There goes the greatest hitter of all time!"

"Teddy Ball Game" does something he never ever does; just before he gets into the car, he turns and tips his hat to me. I feel as if I were on the top of the world. Real joy, even just a few minutes, is truly wonderful. I'm thrilled to have spent some time with my hero.

Ted swore he would never tip his cap for anyone: not his teammates, the fans, and especially the press. I wave to him as he disappears in a new Cadillac up Jersey Street. Walking over to hitch up my Sunshine to the leash, I grab her collar and feel something rolled around the top. It's a twenty-dollar bill.

I smile, feeling grateful; Sunshine and I will do well with this money. Maybe head over to the diner for a steak dinner along with all the "fixins." My mouth waters at the thought.

But, nope, let's tuck this away for later, maybe get a coffee and break the twenty into smaller denominations; that way, it will be broken up if I'm to lose some. *That's a good idea.*

My feet are tired. I find a newspaper in the gutter, take out one page, and fold it until it fit the inside of my shoe. "Yes, Sunshine, this will do for today."

I decided to take the Green Line trolley from Kenmore station to Park Street. There we can get a feel for the lay of the land, so to speak, for tonight's sleeping arrangements.

Chapter 29

DISASTER

The trolley bounces back and forth as it makes its way to Park Street. I feel terrific. I not only met the "Splendid Splinter," but had time and conversation with him. We get off at Park Street and found today's Record American on a bench. It's well into the evening rush hour now, and Sunshine and I decide to do some people-watching, read the paper, and reflect on the day.

It was warm and comfortable down in the T in the wintertime, cool and pleasant in the summer. I have often heard people talk about how the smell is not pleasant. I kind of enjoy the fragrance. Although it is hard to describe to anyone what the subway smells like. I guess the best way to describe it is the smell of dirt, well, the Earth, metal from the rails and trains, and the many perfumes people wear. All in all, not bad. It sure beats the smell of a foxhole in the Pacific.

The time passes quickly. I read most of the paper, I think. One of the crazy stories was the Russians sending a satellite in space. I tip my head back and fell asleep. I'm woken by a group of teenagers laughing at me, calling me a few names.

"Hey, you bum, get a job!"

That's always an easy one to shrug off.

"Why don't you and your bitch get out of the station and let everyone else use it? You smell!"

Words don't hurt much anymore. I am used to most insults. It's mostly the laughter that cuts to the bone. The group of four young men begins throwing coins at Sunshine and me. They look like they may be in high school or even college. Well-dressed, all of them. I can tell they come from money. They come closer and closer. I put my hands up to deflect the coins from hitting my face; at the same time, I tuck Sunshine behind my legs. She's getting scared, and so am I.

"Hey, you stumblebum, go on and get out of here," one of the young men shouts from the back of the pack.

"We want this bench," says the bigger of the four men. He leans in toward my face. "Man, oh man, this guy's breath is worse than a dog's ass," he shouted back to the rest.

I say nothing. Most times when people stare, whisper, I pretend not to notice. Fortunately, or not, I seem to hear and see everything around me. Being aware of my surroundings, I keep a watch with never making eye contact for too long.

The laughter continues, getting louder with each insult. I had hoped they would have their fun and move on. Instead, I can see that I need to get up and away. Just as I turn to gather up everything, a sharp blow comes to the side of my right face, just above the temple. The pain is intense—I fall onto the bench and then the station floor. Sunshine growls, and in a flash, I feel her pull the leash to attack my assailant.

One of the other young men comes over to help his

friend get away from my protector. Sunshine is barking, biting, growling louder even more. *She can bark after all.* I raise my head, feeling the blood drip down. I put out my hand to block a blow from the assailant's foot. I'm only partially successful. People are coming over to see what the commotion is, and I can hear a police whistle in the background.

I have a flashback to a time during the war when I was always ready for battle. My gun, hands, legs, feet, and anything I needed to use to stay alive, I did. So many other soldiers did the same. Now I am not the man I once was. My reflexes are barely enough to stop a shod foot. Could I have fought this young man? Maybe if I tried, I would take a more significant beating by all of them. It might have been worth it for me to stick up for myself, stop the hurled insults and abuse. Instead, I took the beating as my dog stepped up for me.

I begin to feel pain, tears, from being so much less than once I was.

"What's going on here?"

Slowly I make my way back to sitting up.

"This bum's dog started to bite us, so we were defending ourselves," one of the boys yelled out. "Look, see, look." He points to his right arm. "This mutt ripped my jacket and sleeve. She may have even broken the skin. I have to get a rabies shot now."

The transit officer looks at me with sadness and disdain. He puts his nightstick back into his belt. I know he has seen me around before.

A voice far away shouts, "Okay, folks, let's all move along," as the next trolley comes into the station. In a flash, the people who'd watched my beating disappear on their way. No one wants to get involved, not even the

Transit Police. Too much paperwork for the police to deal with, especially if it's a bum that got beat up. This always resonates with me, if I were a stand-up citizen, you best believe there would be reports, arrests. For me and my brethren on the streets, we are not worth the ink and paper.

I sit for a moment in a daze. Why has this happened today, of all days? I met my hero only to have that all taken away by who I am. A bum.

Every time a good thing happens in my day, it's cancelled out by another equally bad moment. My heart aches to have a place to disappear to.

Just like that, it's all over. My assailants get on the trolley, laughing as I make my way back onto the bench.

"Do you want me to get an ambulance to have you checked out?"

I look at the officer for a moment, hold my hand to my head to check on the bleeding. I see his name and badge.

"No, thank you, Officer Bell. I just need a minute, and we will be on our way."

"Okay, buddy, get yourself set up. I have to have you clear out of here in five minutes."

Reaching in my bag for some napkins to hold against my head, I find the white napkins from Joe & Nemo's. Pressing firmly on my head, they keep most of the blood from running down my neck.

I pat Sunshine with my other hand. She's upset and comes over to lick up the blood on my hand and neck. My protector is now a nurse. I laugh sarcastically at my plight, my life, and where I have ended up: on the subway floor, beat up by a man half my age. Not a soul coming to help me but my dog. How pathetic I turned out to be.

Then I feel around Sunshine's body to make sure she's not hurt; she seemed okay.

"Are you ready?" The transit officer makes sure we leave the station and go on our way.

Chapter 30

INVISIBLE

The cold wind meets up with the warm air from the station as I open the door and walk out onto the sidewalk. Then, zipping up my jacket, holding onto my friend, we're off.

How did living, life, friends, and family change so? I think to myself as we slowly, with no direction, walk on.

My job had been okay. I'd had a roof over my head, a few bucks in my pocket, and the promise of a new world. You never know what or where you will end up. I remember the words my mom would often say: "There but for the grace of God go I." They're ringing in my head.

I remember walking by men like me when I was a child.

It was a hot Saturday mid-morning in the summer, and I was walking with my mom on Broadway in Southie. The sidewalk was bustling with shoppers coming and going. We would often go to Broadway for food, clothing, or just a day out.

I think I was around six or seven. It can be hard to place a year and age when I look back. But I know that I was young and holding onto your mom's hand was always in fashion.

Up ahead, I could hear coins rattling in a metal cup—and a man's voice shouting. Mom and I walked on as I tried to see up ahead. I peeked through the legs of people crisscrossing when I saw a man sitting on the sidewalk.

My eyes grew wide. I had never seen anything like this before. I was shocked.

"Don't stare," Mom said sternly, pulling my hand.

I had stopped to see where the noise was coming from. I saw a man rattling a tin cup that held coins and pencils. Pulling away from my mom's soft grip, I walked a few steps in his direction.

"Pencils, pencils, only penny apiece," the man shouted out. He shook his beat-up metal cup side-to-side, trying to get noticed. His voice got louder as people came closer to him.

I had never seen a person look so bad. His hands were dirty, his face tanned, sweaty from the sun. The brown shirt he wore was sweat stained, untucked, and ripped. I noticed he had no socks on. Worn-out shoes and black pants completed his ensemble.

His outstretched right arm waved back and forth, the hand clenched firmly around the tin cup handle. The pencils swam violently around, making noise as they hit each other and the side of the cup. Watching for a few seconds, I was amazed to see that none of the pencils flew away. His left hand lay on his lap, palm up—it looked to be lame, not really formed like his right hand.

The most unsettling thing was that he was blind. I had never seen a blind person before. I stared and watched how his eyes moved, differently than anyone else I had ever seen. Thoughts swam in my mind. *How is this possible? Why is this happening?* I had never seen an adult sitting on the sidewalk—that was one thing grown-ups did not do. But here in front of me was clearly a man in distress. Why was no one helping him? Were we blind to him? Why was no one buying his pencils? My heart ached. This was a new pain which I knew I had never felt before.

"Come along," my mom said, "let's be going."

I held firm as she pulled my arm.

I looked up at her. "Can we buy a pencil?"

She smiled at me as she reached into her purse and found two pennies.

"Here," she said, putting the coins in the palm of my hand.

I walked over slowly and casually to where the man sat begging against the building.

"Here you go, mister." Not knowing how to stop his cup from swinging about I spoke up a bit louder. "Mister, mister!"

Pausing to let me drop in pennies, he smiled at me and said, "Thank you."

I felt wonder, peace, and a connection—to what I had no idea. Trying to look into his eyes I could feel, at least I thought I could feel his pain as well as all that was good in the world. This emotion or feeling of calm in the storm of people all around me lasted for a brief second or two, as the sounds of the world went away. Not knowing what was going on, my mom called me back. I was again in the world.

"Pencils, pencils," he shouted.

Walking back to my mom, holding her hand, she smiled at me and said, "There but for the grace of God go I."

Our walk home made me think of the other side of the world, the other side of living—feelings I had never experienced before.

When we got home, I went straight to my room and pulled out my treasure chest. The old cigar box my dad had given me held all my life savings: nickels, quarters, dimes, lots of pennies, and now two pencils. I closed the lid and slid it back under my bed. It was noontime, and the bells at St. Bridget's tolled.

Chapter 31

KINDNESS

Sunshine and I are hankering to find some food. The cafeteria I like is just a few blocks away and would be a place to spend some of the Splendid Splinter's twenty dollars.

A soup and a sandwich would make a great meal. I'm able to sneak Sunshine into the cafeteria at Summer and Winter streets without the owner noticing. A few patrons are having a late supper. Everyone sits quietly away from each other. The dinner rush is mostly over. I tie her leash loosely to the table leg and scooch her under a chair. Placing the tray on the rail, I slowly walk by the station where some of the food would be in the bin in a few hours. The once-filled-to-the-top soup tureens are almost empty; the rims of where soup has been looks like layers of rocks from the Grand Canyon.

The chicken noodle soup looks good. I reach for the big soup ladle and fill a bowl to the top. I grab a bunch of saltine crackers; some go on the tray, the rest into my pocket. Emily Post, the famous American author on manners and etiquette, writes that you are only supposed to take two packages. Hmmm. I think to myself that I will honor her request if Emily comes by here someday.

Pausing just for a moment, I savor the smells of the many soups. They all smell so good—I take deep breaths in so I can enjoy this event in my mind later.

There are sandwiches all made up, covered with saran wrap to keep them fresh. My eyes dart around till I find ham and cheese. A cup of Joe will make this night complete. Heading toward the cashier, I passed by the desserts. Nope, not tonight. "Let's save our money," I whisper to myself.

"Hello, sweetie."

I smile back to the young lady sitting up on what would be best described as a bar stool-type chair. She smiles and says, "Will that be all for tonight?"

"Ahh, yes." I smile back. "Please, yes, thank you." Unfortunately, I stumble for the right words."

"That will be eighty-five cents."

I give her my Ted Williams twenty-dollar bill. Just like I'd forgotten how nice it is to have a conversation other than begging, I now remember how it feels to have paper money.

"Here you go." She begins to give me my change. I see her look at my hand. Pulling my jacket over my shirt cuffs, I tried in vain to hide some of my uncleanness. I feel shame, embarrassment. *How bad does my face look from that punch? How badly do I smell?*

She can see the panic in my face. Being kind, she pretends that she made a mistake with the change.

"I'm—wait." She pauses. "I have been making so many mistakes today. Let me check that again." Laughing softly to herself, her kind smile makes me smile back. "So here you go." Placing coins and paper money on the tray, she thanks me and wishes me a good night.

I smile bigger for her understanding. "Thank you." I walk back down to where Sunshine sits quietly.

Sitting in my chair, I nudge Sunshine farther under the table and close to the wall. My intention is for no one to see a dog in a restaurant. Pulling apart the sandwich, I toss it to her as quietly as possible. Sipping on the hot soup, I look over at the cashier and think I should have told her the story of my twenty dollars. Would she care that the twenty dollars had once belonged to the "Kid"?

I think better of myself for not telling such a story. It sounds crazy even to me when I think of it now. Who cares whose money it once was? But how I miss conversations, even the silliest ones.

Real, warm food, not from the local mission, tastes so much better. The soup is not watered down and the sandwiches have more than one piece of meat. I rattle and scrape my spoon all around the bowl, getting every drop I can. Getting ready to leave, I pick up the change from the tray and count it; the amount comes to a dollar. The paper money comes to nineteen. The kind lady let me have my dinner for free. I sit quiet for a moment and wait to catch the cashier's eye. She looks up at me as I wave and mouth a "thank you" to her. She smiles back and goes back to reading her book, waiting for the next customer to check out.

Looking down at my hands I notice some of the dried blood is still on the top of my right hand. I thought I had washed all of this away with the napkins from Joe & Nemo's. I feel embarrassed. I guess this is why I got a free meal. If you look like you had been in a boxing match and lost, you get a free dinner.

I laugh at such a silly idea. It was just the lady being kind. Dipping a napkin into the half-filled water glass, I try discreetly to clean up my face and hands from the wound on my head.

Sunshine whimpers a bit. She looks up and tilts her head, knowing as always when I am in distress.

"It's okay, girl," I whisper to her and pat her head. "Let's get a move on." I wave back to the lady at the counter, and she returns the wave and a smile.

It's time to find a place to stay. I think it best not to go to the same subway station; my attackers might come back. I have a sense of dread that takes me back to the Pacific, in the thick jungle. You just know, somehow, that heading into that part of the unknown the enemy is lying in wait to ambush you. So many times, my sixth sense had saved me.

It's a short walk back to the Common. I feel good, different somehow—content would be a better word. Maybe it was the soup and coffee, I can't tell. Sunshine and I go over to the bandstand in the middle of the Common. This is as good a place as any to sleep.

The church bells in the not too far-off distance toll ten. I kick away the broken bottles and debris from the platform. Then I pull out my old couch pillow and blanket and curl up in a ball with Sunshine.

Going to sleep tonight will be difficult with a full belly. It is not something I am used to. Tossing and turning, I have to get up for a while. Sunshine barely moves as I sit on the bandstand stairs and gaze up at the stars.

Chapter **32**

DAD

Bums, low-lives, vagrants, drifters, down on your luck; there are lots of words, and many more, to describe me.

I remember one time I was with my father, out doing errands of some sort. Mom must have had something very big going on. Dad hated to do any type of shopping. We did not usually walk along the streets to get to the store; my dad would drive to the destination, then get in and get out for whatever was needed. This particular day, though, we were walking to the store when a man put out his hand asking for help. "Hey, can you—"

My dad, nearly six feet tall, with broad shoulders and a tough demeanor, stiffened up once the beggar asked for help. My father's face turned from calm to a scowl. "Go on, get going. I've got nothing for you, you bum!"

My father's harsh words hanging in the air, the man looked away in shame. My father's words had hurt. They were meant to, perhaps to wake the man up to get a job, as he would say. Those words hurt me, even back then, to the core. It was if they were directed to me somehow. How could the man I looked up to be so cold to someone that needed so little? Where was my father's kindness? I'd felt such empathy, a connection to the stranger.

We were still within earshot of the beggar when my father shouted, "Son, remember this: don't give your hard-earned money to those people. All they do is drink it away. They need to pick themselves up, move on, be responsible."

I could feel the anger in my dad's soul, him not willing to help. How could that be? I had listened to a few stories through the years at our dinner table on how hard it was growing up in my father's family.

"Each day was a struggle in our home. I would head over with my father every Saturday late afternoon to the North End to buy food for the upcoming week. We would buy what was left of the week-old produce that did not sell in the market. Sometimes, if money was very tight, we would help the peddlers break down their carts for free produce. It was hard growing up; never forget to work hard for what you have." He had such disdain for anyone that was "on the dole."

Chapter *33*

BANDSTAND

The stars are beautiful tonight. I can see my breath, but for some reason I don't feel cold. I look over at Sunshine; she is in a deep, twitching-her-paw sleep. For some reason I am not tired, even after everything that's happened today. I guess I'm too wound up to get any sleep. The noise of the city's slowing down. Only a few cars drive down Tremont Street.

I decide to go and sit on the bandstand stairs and think about all that's happened today. Scraping the broken beer bottle glass off the steps, I sit down near the last step and look up to see a clearer view of the half full moon. The city is quiet. No one is in the Common. That's odd—it isn't all that late, and yet no one is around. *Maybe the cold is keeping them inside.*

Thinking of how great it was to see and spend a few minutes with Ted Williams, I shake my head and smile. Then I think of how bad it was to get beat up, and then have a good meal for free thanks to the kindness of the cashier lady. All in all, not a bad day.

A few minutes, maybe more, pass when a man who

looks familiar, walks over and speaks. "Hello. It's a beautiful night out, isn't it," he says, looking to the sky.

"Yes, it is a calm night," I say. "But how can you really tell with those dark glasses on?"

He smiles and says, "I get by."

We both look up at the cloudless sky, seeing the stars twinkle. We make some more small talk about the weather and the upcoming Red Sox season, and then out of the blue the stranger asks, "I know this is a bit forward of me to ask, but how long have you been on the streets? Do you go to the shelters when you can? I'm sorry if this seems out of place."

I look the man up and down and think, *what the hell. It's someone to talk to.*

My newfound friend sits down on the first step, just below me. He's far enough away from me for me to be comfortable, just in case any funny business is at hand. I can hear Sunshine snoring above, and it makes me feel safe that she doesn't feel threatened.

"Are you a reporter?" I ask.

"Well, sort of. I do make out reports, as you say, but they don't make it to the newspapers."

I thought he must work for the city or the state. Maybe taking an account to see how many men are on the streets in the winter?

"Let me—if again, I may, without getting too personal—ask how you got to be here." He points to the area in front of me and then waves his arms all around.

Pausing to gather my thoughts, I say, "I wasn't always a bum. I had a job, friends, money, and a future. A few bad breaks, the battle with the bottle for a time. I wasn't tossed out by a lady, just took a few wrong turns, and well, I guess I gave up. Like everything that happens to you in life, I thought it would be only for a while, just till I got back on my feet again. I came to find out how easy it was to give up."

I can see the man is listening intently. "Go on," he says.

"Living, or better said, surviving without a home and job is exhausting. I am always tired, cold, hungry, dirty. Even on summer nights it is freezing in Boston. I tried the flophouses, but they are awful. The screams of men from memories of the war or detoxing are constant. Everyone steals from each other. Not to mention how filthy the places are. No, it's much cleaner and, for the most part, safer on the streets. Besides, if I were to find a shelter I would not have my best friend, Sunshine."

My reporter friend chimes in, "Yes, your dog, whom I can hear snoring." He laughs.

"Yup," I say, "they don't let any four-legged creatures in. I tried a few times at different locations, and I always got the 'no dogs allowed' speech.

"Excuse me, but aren't you going to take any notes?" I ask intently. I think that maybe this guy is a bit crazy. Why is he out here tonight, in the cold? Is this man just as crazy as I am?

"No, I'm very good at remembering everything people say," he says, and smiles at me confidently.

I go on a bit more. "What is really difficult about being a beggar is seeing people you once knew from your childhood. It is the most embarrassing thing I have had happen to me. I could elaborate a little on this if you want?"

"I have all the time in the world, go on," he says.

Chapter 34

CATHY

This happened just last month, before Christmas. It must have been around mid-December. Jordan Marsh had the Christmas village out on display in all their huge front windows. I always loved seeing that when I was a child. Lights were hung from one building to the next in celebration of the Christmas Season. Each store had holiday songs playing, and some even cast the music via speakers onto the streets. If you were not in the spirit of the season, all you needed to do was spend a few minutes downtown and that would surely change.

It was a Saturday morning; the hustle and bustle of shoppers were in full swing at the downtown crossing. The weather was perfect—not too cold, no snow, and best of all, the sun was shining. I had panhandled that morning, making a good haul. 'Tis the season, ho-ho-ho, as they say. Maybe I'd even go into Jordan Marsh for some hot blueberry muffins before the day was over.

Sunshine and I needed a stretch of the legs. *Let's go and see this year's Christmas display.* Strolling, but keeping our distance from the shoppers, I paused at one of Santa's workshop windows.

It had been many years since I last laid eyes on Santa's workshop in the windows. *They are still as lovely as I remembered. I'm not sure if they've ever changed.* "They must have," I whispered. I had not realized that I had spoken out loud. A nearby lady dressed smartly in her red coat turned in my direction. She was holding her daughter's hand.

I looked toward her—it was Cathy. My sweetheart, the only girl I had ever loved.

She looked at me, and then I think she tried unsuccessfully to look beyond me for a quick second. Then, finally, her beautiful brown eyes lit up her face. Cathy looked terrific. It was as if she had not aged at all. Her daughter, maybe nine or ten, asked, "Who is this, Mommy?"

"Hello, Cathy," I said as I took off my hat.

"Hello … " Before Cathy could respond and say my name, I interrupted her.

"I'm a friend of your mom from an awfully long time ago." I reached my hand out to her daughter. "My name is—" Just then, Sunshine spoke up. With a little yelp, she jumped up to say hi.

"This is my girl, her name is Sunshine, and she is the very best of dogs. She wants to greet you if that's okay. She is my angel. Once she knows people are safe, she loves to become their friends."

"I'm Mary," the girl said to Sunshine. She came close enough to pat her on her head and talk to her.

I could see and feel how uneasy Cathy felt. She whispered, "How did this happen to you? What, I can't … " Words seemed to flow together, making no sense. Cathy was visibly upset, trying to hide as much as she could from her daughter.

"Mister, your dog is lovely. Mommy, why can't we have a dog?"

"No, dear, we can't have a dog," Cathy quipped back to Mary.

"I'm sorry that you had to see me this way. Not sure how this happened. It's not permanent, just a time I am in until life gets a bit better." These were true lies, not the white lies all of us on the streets tell ourselves each day. *It's only temporary till I get back on my feet. A job is right around the corner.* All lies.

Tears were filling Cathy's eyes. "I don't know what to say. I'm so sorry," she said. Then, reaching for a tissue in her purse, she tried to make sure she was discreet so as not to alarm her daughter that she was upset.

"You have nothing to be sorry for. This is what and where my life is right now. It is okay." I looked into her eyes, trying to assure her that I was alright.

Cathy began to reach into her purse again. Not for a tissue but for money. I put my hand up, smiled, and whispered firmly, "No."

"Well, Sunshine, let us be off for another adventure." I pulled her leash back to me. "Ladies, it was beautiful seeing both of you. I want to wish you both the absolute best Christmas."

Mary smiled and wished us both a Merry Christmas. Cathy stood silent. I doffed my hat to them both and walked to the other side of the street.

I glanced at the reflection in the glass window as Sunshine and I quickly walked away. I could see Cathy and Mary stroll along, looking at the rest of the displays.

My heart, with all its feelings for Cathy, was again ripped open. I felt so alone. I had no idea how much in love I still was. That was by far one of the most challenging days in my life. All those nights alone sleeping on the streets, and that empty feeling, missing life, friends, and the only girl that I had ever really loved. I had so much wanted me to be the one with Cathy.

Would Mary be my daughter? Would I have had more kids? Thoughts screamed in my head; my heart pounded as if it were going to burst with sadness. Tears began to well up in my eyes as Sunshine and I hurried up Winter Street, ducking into a coffee shop, not caring if they yelled at me for bringing in a dog.

"How's that for a story," I ask the reporter.

"Very hard on you, I can see. You had a rough patch, many rough patches," he says in a consoling voice.

Chapter *35*

ANGELS

It feels so good to talk, to explain what I have been through. "It's all part of being alone," I say further, "the heaviness of being alone and on the street is a constant drain on your soul."

Taking a long deep breath in, I tilt my head and sigh out with a long exhale, looking at the night sky. I feel peace and inner quiet in my mind like I never have before.

"Do you have other homeless friends out here?" he asks.

"No, not really. They come and go. Once in a blue moon, I make my way to Filene's Basement for some new clothes when I have a few dollars. I trust a few guys to watch Sunshine when I do. Not ever trying to get too close to anyone out here. It seems when I do, just like in the service they end up dead. Or worse, you never find out if they made it off the streets."

"What else do you … what I mean is, during your day, when you're panhandling, what do you see, what do you feel?"

"What do you mean by feel?" I ask.

My friend smiles and kindly says, "What do you feel when people walk by? Could you sense their pain, feel joy and sadness, maybe anger and joy? These were not your feelings—you were in tune and connected with them when you looked into their eyes. You saw the souls of each person."

I never thought anyone knew that I felt, could feel the city: its souls, its heartbeat. I was never sure what the feeling was. I thought myself going mad at times to even think I could feel anything.

Pausing for a minute to collect my thoughts I say in a questioning voice, "I did, though. I thought those were my feelings, my emotions. I make that connection just for a brief moment when I look into their eyes." I smile at him. "How did you know that? Were you once like me?"

He laughs, and says, "Well, not really. Not in that sense you mean. Do you believe in God? I already know the answer to that question, strike that. Let me put it to you this way. We all have tasks in life—jobs, if you will. Most of us go through life working, taking care of our families the best we know how. That's their plan; others have different plans or end up on different paths. It's not always what we would hope for in our lives. When we die, we hope the scales are in our favor to be in the presence of God. Most of us hope that we will be in Heaven. That is a lovely plan, and it works for so many of us."

I listen intently to this story; I can see that there is more.

"Since the beginning of mankind, God has put 'keepers of the flame,' if you will, on this Earth. They are the forgotten ones, cast outs. Are you familiar with the Bible?" he asks.

"Some parts. Not chapter and verse, but I know most of the stories. Are you a preacher, or priest of some sort?" I ask, beginning to feel anxious.

"Not in that sense. Let me tell you a part of the Bible that will apply here, sort of. It goes along the lines of …

> *As Jesus approached Jericho, a blind man was sitting by the roadside begging. When he heard the crowd going by, he asked what was happening. They told him, "Jesus of Nazareth is passing by." He called out, "Jesus, Son of David, have mercy on me!" Those who led the way rebuked him and told him to be quiet, but he shouted all the more, "Son of David, have mercy on me!" Jesus stopped and ordered the man to be brought to him. When he came near, Jesus asked him, "What do you want me to do for you?" "Lord, I want to see," he replied. Jesus said to him, "Receive your sight; your faith has healed you." Immediately he received his sight and followed Jesus, praising God. When all the people saw it, they also praised God.*

"Depending on which part of scripture you choose to believe, that was how it went, that is. But it is much more than that story."

The man told such a good yarn I had to keep listening.

"You were selected to be one of the many watchful eyes for God on Earth. Men and women from the beginning of time have been where you are. They, you, become eyes of God. God does see all. God wants, needs, to have souls on the streets literally feeling the pulse of the world. In every part of the globe we have forgotten souls of all ages, races, creeds. They see from the ground up, as you have, how the world is."

I'm stunned; this guy must be crazy—such a story. God needs souls or eyes on the ground, how ridiculous.

My new friend looks at me a bit more intently. "Don't you remember how each time you hear the church bell chime, you pause, close your eyes just for a moment, and feel a release? Your soul feels lighter, a burden lifted? Think back on those times. You were connected to God— just for a moment, he was there with you and you with him. You gave him an accounting each time the bells rang."

I can feel my jaw dropping as he tells these fantastic tales.

"I'm not saying that God is not with us every second of the day, I'm really not. But what you and so many people have is a bond, unlike the rest, to feel pain, sorrow, happiness, joy, and so much more. You watch people come and go. You feel for God. I know you believe in Angels, bad and good. They are here on Earth and all around us; we just don't see them. God has a job for them as well. Your job is different but no less critical."

What is this man talking about? My mind is spinning as he goes on turning this tale. I must be getting on. I start to get up but pause. I feel different. A profound peace is coming over me.

"Do you remember Father Mike and how he lifted your heavy burden? How about Mae, her kindness and compassion to you? How about your brothers in arms, how you kept each other safe? Most of all, your mom, and how she gave you the guide for life. How peaceful, close to God you felt when you were with her. How about Ted Williams, a man that never tipped his cap for anyone and yet he did for you.

"Some people we meet during our life we have an

instant connection with. Others we meet just in passing; we are not meant to be in their universe. We hardly notice them as they walk on by."

How can this man know my life? Is this a dream? It's all too much for me to comprehend.

Chapter 36

PAIN

The squeal from the trolley's iron wheels on the iron track deafens my pleas. "Stop, stop," I shout out, my head pounding, pain radiating over my whole body.

One young man smiles as he lifts his leg, his shoe heading for Sunshine. I plead, shout, "No, don't, please don't kick my dog—" Another punch, a kick from the other two men hits me hard. The remnants of beer bottles are poured over me as fists strike my side and break my ribs. The last young man in the group of four watches, smiling at me. He waits for his turn to join in on the fun, cheering the other three on as they circle me.

I am now on my knees, pleading for them all to stop, covering up myself and Sunshine as best as I can. These men love giving me and Sunshine a beating; their laughter is sinister.

Sunshine growls, snaps, and yelps in pain all in one breath. She tries to bite, but a weak snarl is all she had left. Pleading is hard; I can't catch my breath with my broken ribs. I lost track of the fourth man, somehow. He gets behind me and with one mighty strike on the back of my head, I fall to the platform floor. Before I pass out, I hear my front teeth shatter on the cement.

I know I'm only out for a second or so. The blood pouring out of my mouth and pain over my whole body wakes me up. My tongue frantically searches for teeth that are no longer there. Sunshine is wobbling, looking like she's going to fall. The young men are laughing, pouring more beer over me and Sunshine.

"Here you go, you bum." One more kick and Sunshine yelps and falls next to me. I can see life slipping out of her eyes. Reaching my arm over, I try in vain to pull her close to me, but it's too late to save her. My body in so much pain—all I can do is cry for Sunshine. Muffled noises in the background come closer.

"Get an ambulance, quick," someone shouts.

Chapter *37*

HEAVEN'S WINDOW

My friend's voice has changed; it is more direct but reassuring.

"God chose you, before you were born to see, to feel all that is good on the Earth, and all that is not. You were his eyes from the ground up. Now it's time to come along with me." The man's hand reaches for mine.

I look closer at him. The moonlit sky shows his face clearer now. He seems so familiar.

"Hey, aren't you the man from Joe & Nemo's"?

"Yes, I am," he says confidently.

"I knew you were, you looked so familiar to me," I say in a very relieved voice.

"Take my arm if you will, please," he requests. "It's time to go."

I feel obliged to do so. But just before I do, I shout, "Sunshine, girl, come on." I whistle two short bursts.

"It's okay. She will be along soon enough," he says softly. I look at my new friend. He pauses, takes off his glasses, smiles, and says to me, "By the way, I want to thank you for the two pennies. There but for the grace of God go I. Beautiful words your mom once said."

I reach for his arm, feeling at total peace.

"How about a stroll over to the Public Garden before we leave? What would you say to that?"

I smile and nod as we walk through the Common. The world is still. I can smell the fresh-cut grass. I see the flowers beginning to bloom as we get close to the Public Garden. A soft rain begins to fall, and in the distance I see Sunshine running toward me as the church bells chime.

About the Author

Bill Selvitelle grew up in Boston—better said Southie and Dorchester. He married his childhood sweetheart. They had two sons, one who passed due to Aortic Aneurysm from his undiagnosed Marfan Syndrome when he was fourteen. Bill retired from Eversource after thirty-nine years. He currently teaches yoga four times a week on Green Harbor Beach, Marshfield, Massachusetts, to help the local food pantry. His mission now is going into Boston when he has spare clothing or food to help our homeless brothers and sisters.

Writing has been a passion of Bill's for many years. *Heaven's Window* is his first novel.

Heaven's Window

Bill Selvitelle

Publisher: SDP Publishing
Also available in ebook format

 SDP Publishing

www.SDPPublishing.com
Contact us at: info@SDPPublishing.com

www.ingramcontent.com/pod-product-compliance
Lightning Source LLC
Chambersburg PA
CBHW031606260626
47154CB00020B/1642